Legendary Tales

Edited By Xena-Jo Draper

First published in Great Britain in 2022 by:

Young Writers
Remus House
Coltsfoot Drive
Peterborough
PE2 9BF
Telephone: 01733 890066
Website: www.youngwriters.co.uk

Printed and bound in the UK by BookPrintingUK
Website: www.bookprintinguk.com
YB0512J

Foreword

Welcome Reader!

Are you ready to discover strange and wonderful creatures that you'd never even dreamed of?

For Young Writers' latest competition 'Bonkers Monsters', we asked primary school pupils to create a creature of their own invention, and then write a story about it using just 100 words - a hard task! However, they rose to the challenge magnificently and the result is this fantastic collection full of creepy critters and amazing animals!

Here at Young Writers our aim is to encourage creativity in children and to inspire a love of the written word, so it's great to get such an amazing response, with some absolutely fantastic stories.

Not only have these young authors created imaginative and inventive monsters, they've also crafted wonderful tales to showcase their creations. These stories are brimming with inspiration and cover a wide range of themes and emotions - from fun to fear and back again!

I'd like to congratulate all the young authors in this anthology, I hope this inspires them to continue with their creative writing.

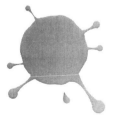

Contents

Lockers Park School, Hemel Hempstead

Leon Vandra-Simon (11)	58
German Pankov (11)	59
Andrey Pavlov (10)	60
Matthew Lewis (10)	61
Jonathan Elia (10)	62
Thomas Pinchin (10)	63

Macaulay CE Primary School, Clapham

Teni Bamigboye (9)	64
Imogen Kempsey (9)	65
Ava Toemehn (9)	66
Milly Andrews (9)	67
Lola Hodges (9)	68
Brooklyn Harper (8)	69
Theo Swash (9)	70
Eve Reid (8)	71
Eleanor Whittle (9)	72

Mossend Primary School, Bellshill

Amelie Nisbet (6)	73
Finnlay Nisbet (6)	74
Caoimhe Rooney (7)	75
Ellie Mullin (7)	76
Olivia van den Berg (6)	77
Isla Mae Currie (7)	78
Isla Liddell (5)	79
Taylor Campbell (5)	80

St Joseph's Catholic Primary School, Northfleet

Faith Vaja (6)	81
Elliot Hodge (9)	82
Temilayo Adesina (8)	83
Emily Chama (7)	84
Maryam Sassou (9)	85
Mikie Brown-Deane (7)	86
Kyra Manan (8)	87
Annie Bennett (7)	88

Tilly Byrne (10)	89
Ethne Scullion-Smith (11)	90
Jayden Kyle Botwe (6)	91
Raiya Nair (6)	92
Sophie Wisniewska (7)	93
Anaiya Rodriques (7)	94
India Keeble (11)	95
Tayla Mark-Ihama (7)	96
Ruby Timlin (6)	97
Jeremy Pulik (7)	98
Iris Rea (8)	99
Eitan Adekunle-Adebayo (7)	100
Kehinde Adekunle (6)	101

Three Bridges Primary School, Three Bridges

Evie Connell (8)	102
Abdullah Umair (7)	103
Harvey Kelsey (8)	104
Ogooluwa Folami (7)	105
Aishani Chowdhuri (9)	106
Ishana Verma (7)	107
Anjana Theepan (8)	108
Alex Emmans (8)	109
Joshua Callaghan (8)	110
Ricky-Lee	111
Alice Larkins (8)	112
Rio Rajack (9)	113
Delroy Tewe (7)	114
Ashley Retter (8)	115
Daniel Tanimowo (7)	116
Krupa	117
Aminata Ndiaye (8)	118
Nathan H (8)	119
Lily Grimley (8)	120
Amirah Shah (8)	121
Abhijeet Dale (9)	122
Emma Devoil (8)	123
Leela Withers (8)	124
Lainey Browne (7)	125
Harley Redwood (7)	126
Jayden Hanna (9)	127
Ayaan Farooque (8)	128

Leo Trinidad (8)	129	Mahi	172
Kenzie Oliver (8)	130	Lacey (8)	173
Avleen Kaur Wahla (8)	131	Max Roper (8)	174
Adam Timms (8)	132	Robbie Irving (8)	175
Yusuf Shah (8)	133	Zaine-King Burrows (7)	176
Aaminah Akiyas (8)	134	Lenny Kemsley (7)	177
Tanisha Bhimjiani (8)	135		
Owais Rahman (8)	136		
Harjit Thiagarajan (9)	137		

Uplands Junior School, Wolverhampton

Sothia	138	Harley Bladen-Hayes (10)	178
Alexander Nosenko (8)	139	Elsa McMurtrie (11)	179
Finn Rina	140	Martha Taylor-Ashcroft (10)	180
Jacob Drummond (7)	141	Charlie Moulsdale (10)	181
Aizan Ailaz (7)	142	Ava Rutter (10)	182
Freya Sharman (7)	143	Laila Montague (8)	183
Kayla Laignau (7)	144	Mason Russello-Nar (9)	184
Muhammad Abdullah (9)	145	Sienna Kumari (10)	185
Amelia Gillam (8)	146	Lucy Amelia Brown (10)	186
Ritojit Mukhopadhyay (8)	147	Carrum Sekhon (9)	187
Mika Rifky Mohamed (8)	148	Jasmin Sandhu (9)	188
Ashley Ditzel (8)	149	Beatrice Machin (9)	189
Nathan Bottazzini	150	Acira Kumar (9)	190
Sam Patel (7)	151	Jessica Morgan	191
Sarunya Thamilmaran (8)	152	Aadreyi Chattopadhyay (9)	192
Morgan Myburgh (8)	153	Lewis Hitch (10)	193
Yavan Murugaraj (9)	154	Georgia Winwood (8)	194
Nithin Nadane (8)	155	Abigail Shepherd (8)	195
Eman Aijaz (7)	156		
Kaidee Hanna	157		
Surriyah-Rose Jock Miller (8)	158		
Maayah Jameela Khan (8)	159		
Milan Kadar (8)	160		
Harry Makepeace (8)	161		
Anastasia Eleonore (9)	162		
Aimee Murray (7)	163		
Zainab Farooq (7)	164		
Galiene Natalie Sebide (8)	165		
Lamya Razi Mohamed (7)	166		
Eliza Iotu (8)	167		
Timea Kery-Toth (8)	168		
Caleb Thorn (8)	169		
Zayn Amin (8)	170		
Mia Roper (9)	171		

The
Stories

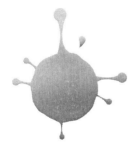

Cupcake's Out Of Their World Adventure

As her eyes slowly opened, Cupcake looked around at the unfamiliar surroundings. *Where am I?* she thought to herself, scratching her head. Cupcake appeared to be in a gloomy rainforest, but how she got there, Cupcake had no idea. Deciding to explore, Cupcake wandered around for a while, passing terrifying trees, abnormal animals and even purple plants. The further she went, the more confusing things got. Without warning, Cupcake's vision blurred and a distant ringing in her ears grew louder and louder. *Boom!* Cupcake opened her eyes to find herself very cosy in her bed. Was it all a dream?

Zuzanna Gacka (11)
Croft Junior School, Stockingford

Face Your Problems

Ring! "There's the bell, class dismissed!" the teacher shouted. Sunshine the axolotl packed her bag and left the class. She went down the corridor and saw Bill the fish bullying Ollie the octopus. Knowing it was wrong, she walked to the situation calmly, tapped Bill on the shoulder, and said, "Stop!"

Bill glared at her. "What are you gonna do?" he asked sassily.

Sunshine hesitated, she ran and said not a word all day, anxiety was building up each second. Weeks later, she told a teacher about it as well as her anxiety. All was sorted, everyone was happy.

Ella Dadzis (9)
Croft Junior School, Stockingford

Balloooni And The Rise And Fall Of Master Pinner

Balloooni was a bright red, energetic balloon who was not able to fly. He was the only balloon who could deflate and pump himself back up. One warm day, on the sunny planet Helium of the balloon system, Balloooni met his evil arch-nemesis, Master Pinner of the Needles, and decided to go and talk to him. Balloooni explained to him enthusiastically, "I want a battle. Now. Just you and me." Master Pinner nodded obediently. Just then, Balloooni deflated and let out a hissing sound, zooming around and circling Master Pinner, whilst hastily tying him up with his stretchy balloon string.

Freya Lawrence (9)
Croft Junior School, Stockingford

The Day Earth Met Blarg

In a galaxy far away, Blarg lived on Planet Spuce Moose. He has weird but wonderful skills. Blarg turns into stone when he's near lava. When he landed in London, he went shopping for human clothes to blend in. As the cashier looked at him, she screamed, "What do you want?" and fainted. Blarg walked outside. Everyone loved him because when people looked into his eyes, he could control them. So then people loved him. People of Earth asked him to live with them.

"Yes," he replied. Everyone helped him to build a lovely house. Blarg lived happily after that.

Harrison Guise (10)
Croft Junior School, Stockingford

The Wild Woods

One night, in a little cottage, Brooke sat in her bedroom playing with her crystal pendant. All of a sudden, her pendant kept on moving towards the woods. The pitch-black, shadowy woods. She was terrified but thought to herself that she actually fancied an adventure, so she set off. A few minutes later, she arrived. Unfortunately, the gates were shut but that wasn't going to stop Brooke. The full moon came out behind the gloomy, cheerless clouds. That was when she saw someone behind her. A black outlined figure. Was it a person? Was it an animal? What was it?

Ava Sadler (11)
Croft Junior School, Stockingford

Don't Assume Everything!

It was a normal day in Finland, but then there was a very loud noise. As everyone was scared and gasping at one specific person... Scribble, the strongest man there, and as usual, there must always be a twist because Scribble only comes if one person in the world is there. And guess who? Wimmzier! The smart and fastest person on Earth. One day, Scribble was climbing a mountain and found people and he thought he could beat them up, unsuccessfully. He was blasted to space by the orders of Wimmzier Wontomserry... Scribble may be gone but not for long...

Zain Juma (9)
Croft Junior School, Stockingford

The Slime Snail

Once there was a snail called Jeffery, he was known for stealing the most precious jewellery. He was very slimy so he could climb up the stiff rock walls. Meanwhile, the superhero Stretch was travelling to Egypt. In a glimpse of his eye, he saw the snail trying to steal treasure from a pyramid. He chased after him. He entered the pyramid. The traps were constantly intense. Jeffery got his slime trail so Stretch got stuck. Snail got to the treasure and took it. He was about to leave when he got punched, flying into space. Stretch won the fight.

Zak Butler (9)
Croft Junior School, Stockingford

Dance In The Spotlight

Hi, my name is KK McTom and I'm a Canadian dance monster. I love doing street performing to show off my singing, juggling and dancing to earn extra money. Yesterday, Batman started a live Instagram feed, laughing at my dancing which made me very anxious. I fled into a dark alley but Batman followed and started strangling me. I used my many legs to overpower Batman and escape. By morning, I had calmed down and returned to my street performances. Batman's live feed had introduced me to so many new fans who came to watch my show.

Eva-May Cantrill (9)
Croft Junior School, Stockingford

Bozo And Bonfire Night

One bonfire night, Bozo was going to sleep in his underground house when... *Boom!* He was sent rocketing into the sky, finding himself sat on a jet of colourful sparks. He was like a flying bird that was just set free. That was the fun bit but he knew what was ahead... *Thump!* He landed face down on the muddy grass. As he rolled over, he found he had fallen into a vat of dog poo. After a good five minutes of struggling to get out, one thing dawned on Bozo, his house was blown up.
"Not again!" he cried.

Daisy Davis (10)
Croft Junior School, Stockingford

The Story Of Frode

Frode was a monster, a joyful monster. He had emerald skin and sapphire eyes. However, he had a horrible life, he was kept in a cage. However, one day, Frode decided to escape. He smashed his cage open with a hammer that he hid and escaped! Frode was then wandering through the forest that he had found until he came across a river. This river was important because it was the only way home. Frode built a boat. The humans pounced, they tried to stop him, but Frode was far too quick. He rapidly jumped in and escaped safely home.

Isabelle Harcourt (10)
Croft Junior School, Stockingford

Gizmo The Aquatic Dog

Once upon a time, there was a dog called Gizmo. He went on adventures but once on a little adventure, he saw a giant shadow. Gizmo was scared so he hid behind a rock. It was Aquaticalizon. It was a fierce beast, feared by many.

Aquaticalizon water sprouted the rock with electricity. Gizmo ran as far as he could but couldn't escape the wrath of Aquaticalizon. Gizmo gave running up and decided to fight. Aquaticalizon packed a punch but eventually, Gizmo gave the final blow. Back in the town, Gizmo was cheered on.

Nathan Arnold (8)
Croft Junior School, Stockingford

Spu

Once upon a space-time, lived a nice monster. This monster's name was Spu. He lived with a mean family. He was the only kind one. Spu believed that 'what happens in the dark, always comes to the light'. One day, he went to his rocket car and flew to the shop. On the way, he helped so many monsters. When he came back, Spu noticed his family was having bad luck. But Spu was having good luck. His family noticed that he was correct about 'what happens in the dark, always comes to light'. Be kind.

Annabelle Sellick (10)

Croft Junior School, Stockingford

Two Monsters Making Friends In Hawaii

Once upon a time, Sophie was on the beach in Hawaii and saw a girl monster called Sophia. She was very sad because her favourite toy washed away in the sea. Sophie and Sophia met on the beach every day and made sandcastles every day too. Sometimes they played in the sea or they were swimming in the sea. One day, Sophie and Sophia were swimming late at night and the tide came in and Sophie hurt her foot because there was a big rock and she broke her foot. Sophia looked after her and then they became friends.

Gracie-Mai Greenway (8)
Croft Junior School, Stockingford

The Investigation Of The Bonky Wonky Monster

In a land far away, was an underground basement. Bob and Jake were looking for an ancient monster. After a week, it was time to set off. Jake and Bob started at the campsite then they went through the enchanted forest. When they were going through, they went past a barn owl, then a fox. After they came to the bridge of doom, they had to be careful because steps off the bridge might fall. After 100 miles, they had reached the Bonky Wonky monster. But when it scared them, the exhausted travellers ran away.

Tianna Macbeth (7)
Croft Junior School, Stockingford

Planet Earth To Planet Kelper

Once upon a time, Planet Earth didn't have enough resources so they had to find a different planet to get to, but they couldn't decide which one to go to. But then a man said Kelper.

Then another man said, "Kelper, is that even a planet?" Then they all agreed so they went to a rocketship and they all went into space. Then they found Kelper. Then it was like Earth but with more resources. Then they saw a big shadow. It was a monster called Ushioni. He ate everyone.

Blane Tilson (9)
Croft Junior School, Stockingford

Derik The Thief

On a very bright, sunny evening, Gener was playing on his brand-new bicycle in his garden. Then, all of a sudden, he heard someone shouting, "Gener! Gener!" Gener froze. Who's calling his name? He slowly put his bike on the floor and anxiously teleported towards the echoes. He went back to the garden but his bike was gone. Then he realised that his enemy, Derik, had done that. After, he heard Derik yelling, "Loser!" Gener spotted him clumping up the eaves of his house. Gener teleported to him and snatched it off him. Derik has learnt to never steal.

Ishaq Irfan Mohammed (8)
Heathfield Primary School, Handsworth

The Naughty Kingdom

Once upon a time, lived a monster called Da Monsta. This monster was no ordinary monster. He had sharp claws, ginormous teeth and most importantly, magical powers. The monster was evil and loved eating people. Surprisingly, there were loads of monsters. They all were magical. Da Monsta was the king of this kingdom. The only kingdom that had more power was Everest. The king on Everest was called Stephen.

One day, Da Monsta said that a great war would happen between the kingdoms. Stephen agreed for the war to happen. The battle was for seven days. Kingdom Everest won.

Jinan Mohammed (8)
Heathfield Primary School, Handsworth

Tickles And The Lonely Monster

Tickles and his friends are on the space bus to school. They're all chatting and having fun playing games. Tickles sees a pink, furry new friend to make. He goes over to introduce himself. The girl turns her back on him. Tickles is upset but keeps trying. The girl sees his determination to become friends. Her name's Mia and they have fun the whole way. Along the way, Tickles introduces Mia to everyone. Mia has lots of fun with everyone. Tickles achieved his goal. To make no one lonely and have lots of new friends to play with every day.

Imaani Dawood (11)
Heathfield Primary School, Handsworth

The Missing Diamond

One day, Snugglepuff bought a massive diamond. She put it safely by her bed. One day, she was sleeping and three robbers came and stole the shiny diamond. When they stole it, they left. Snugglepuff then woke up and found out it was gone. She realised her window was broken. So she flew out the cave and searched for the diamond. Then she finally found the thief, she flew down to capture her diamond. She caught it and took it back home. Instead of putting it by her bed, she hid it under her bed. So she saved her day.

Mariyam Imaan (9)
Heathfield Primary School, Handsworth

The Missing Family

Once upon a time, there was an egg. Mr and Mrs Ox had to go somewhere so they went. Then the Babos threw the egg away. When Mr and Mrs Ox went, they couldn't find their egg. The egg hatched then the baby's name was Ox because that's what they would name him. As he grew older, he learnt how to be invisible. Suddenly, a gang of Babos started chasing Ox but then he went invisible. They couldn't find him. He fell in the water and the missing baby was found. Mr and Mrs Ox found baby Ox.

Abu-Bakr Mohammad (8)
Heathfield Primary School, Handsworth

Blobina Living In My Pond

Once upon a time, there was a cat screaming in my back garden. I had a look and what I saw was a cat fighting but there was nobody there. In my mind, I was thinking, *that it is strange. Why would a cat do that?* The next day, I woke up, put my shoes on and went to the garden. That's when I met Blobina. The next day, I saw Blobina come out of my pond and the next day, I woke up and the plan worked. I was so happy they were friends and they smiled every day.

Amelia Hamid (8)
Heathfield Primary School, Handsworth

Fluffy Is Gone!

Once upon a time, there was a cute, tiny monster called Fluffy. He was very popular until... it was his birthday. His mom, dad and family surprised him. When he went to the shop, he saw a... hole? Someone purposely pushed him in the hole! On his birthday?! He couldn't get out. He tried calling for help but no one answered... His mom and dad tried calling him but he declined all of them.

Haadia Shakir (9)
Heathfield Primary School, Handsworth

My Life In The Underground

In a beautiful country called England, underground there was a monster called Blobby and his life was miserable. And he never ever had food. He ate slime. He always cried while he ate but he never gave up. He always tried to make money and he did not like that but he kept trying. And he always walked on the streets and everybody looked away. And look at his life. Never ever give up.

Minaal Khan (7)

Heathfield Primary School, Handsworth

The Nice Monster

Once upon a time lived a yeti called Mangi. He had an opposite twin called Angin. He always wanted to tease Mangi. Mangi always tried to stop him but he failed. One day, a weird-looking yeti said a terrible thing. "Your parents, they're gone." Mangi cried while Angin left. He ran away and went to Alaska and saw a lot of penguins and seals. Mangi was wandering in Alaska when he found Angin.

Angin said, "Uh, it's you again."

Mangi asked, "Why don't you like me?"

"Because our parents liked you more," Angin replied. "And I'm sorry."

Imogen Lewis (7)

Junction Farm Primary School, Eaglescliffe

Sir Wallace And His Mischievous Monster

Sir Wallace was a determined young man who was respected in Stockshire. He was accompanied by his mischievous little monster, Scuty. Wallace found Scuty sheltering beneath a rusty bike shed which almost collapsed on him, with his orange head protruding. They were inseparable. They were sent to a village to deal with Edwin the dragon in a nearby cave. It was adorned with crystals that dangled like dandelions in the cave. Inside, a fire breathing dragon swooped upon them ferociously. Scuty and Wallace attacked from behind. After the fight, Wallace and Scuty retreated back to the fortress and were rewarded.

Shourjo Dasgupta (10)
Junction Farm Primary School, Eaglescliffe

Clumsy On His First Day Of School

Clumsy is a colour changing monster from Clever Town. Nervous, he is starting his first day at Bonkers Monsters School. Wanting to make new friends, Clumsy tries to juggle and change colour. Sadly, one of the balls gets caught on his horns and he loses his balance and trips over, smashing the teacher's special cup. Clumsy races to the corner and sobs. All the monsters come and cuddle Clumsy. He picks himself up and starts making a love heart out of the pieces of the smashed cup. "Brilliant!" smiles the teacher. Everyone laughs and makes friends with each other.

Rebecca Daniel (8)
Junction Farm Primary School, Eaglescliffe

The Incredible Laser In The Cave

Once upon a time, there was a happy family. There was a girl called Laser. She was sleepwalking and he woke up and appeared in a cave and was quite scared. But suddenly she saw someone dancing. It was a monster and his name was Maser.

Laser said, "Hi, I'm lost. Can you help me?"

"Of course I'll help you!"

When they went further down to have a good look around there, they were surprised at how big the place was. After walking for endless hours, Laser heard birds chirping at her window. She woke up. It was a dream.

Aaral Kumar (7)

Junction Farm Primary School, Eaglescliffe

All About Boomboo At Horse Riding

Boomboo is going to the incredible horse riding but he was scared so I decided to help him. He still was scared so I taught him. Then I said, "You may or may not get back on at groundwork to regain control." And I reminded him to listen and be respectful. Look, I will show you and Boomboo not to be scared.

1. Work with an instructor or another experienced horse person.
2. Talk to your equestrian friends.
3. Study training material in books and videos.
4. Research horse behaviour and health.
5. Spend time having fun.

Erin Robinson (7)

Junction Farm Primary School, Eaglescliffe

Lucky Lucy

Lucy was invited to a birthday party and was riding there on a bike with the present in her basket. She went down a hill, going faster and faster, but could not stop as the brake did not work. She was going to hit a ragged, majestic birch tree. She used her monster powers and transformed into a humongous, massive monster with wings. She flew into the sky and then *crash!* Lucy was safe but her bike was irreparable. Unfortunately, the present fell into a puddle. What would Lucy do? She saw some colourful flowers. Hooray! The party was saved.

Chloe Wrigley (7)
Junction Farm Primary School, Eaglescliffe

Invisible Rainbow

Once there was a rainbow octopus named Bonnie. She had beautiful scales and she was so graceful. She danced and pranced in her colourful room. Nothing stopped Bonnie. But one day, something did! She woke up and to her surprise, she was turning grey. She was horrified to see herself this ugly. But all that matters is that she was alive. "Ahh," said Bonnie but then Bonnie wanted to hula hoop and it worked. Actually, she was so happy that she jumped so high, that she reached the puffy cotton candy-like clouds. She was really pleased.

Eleanor Bould (7)
Junction Farm Primary School, Eaglescliffe

No Need To Worry!

One gloomy day, Laura was feeling awfully sad, so her mum bought her two monster teddies. Laura ran up to her room delighted. She picked up Gloom-lu and started playing but Laura didn't feel better. She picked up Sophie and she felt miraculously better. Suddenly Gloom-lu started to stand up and all of Laura's nightmares came flooding through her mind. Sophie stood up and picked up Gloom-lu and carried him all the way to the shop and ran back. Laura gasped and said in a daze, "I don't know what to say. Thank you, I guess!"

Scarlett Arrowsmith (11)

Junction Farm Primary School, Eaglescliffe

Bomer And His New Friends

Once upon a time, there was a monster called Bomer. But Bomer was alone and didn't have any friends. One day a rabbit was stuck in a hole. Bomer helped the little rabbit. After Bomer helped the rabbit, the rabbit asked the monster if it was kind. Bomer said yes. The rabbit ran away and told everyone that Bomer was nice. Then there was a monkey stuck in a small tree hole. The monster helped the monkey by pulling. Everyone came and said, "Can you be my friend?" Bomer said yes. So everyone was happy and had lots of fun.

Yuthara Perera (7)
Junction Farm Primary School, Eaglescliffe

The Chick's Life

Once upon a time, a little chick was sleeping on her hay. Suddenly, she heard a noise. It was a scary noise. Just then, the chick realised it was a bear. She was afraid. *Bang!* A bear's hand was in the chick's view.

"Oh no!" whispered the little girl. The girl shooed the bear away. The next day, the girl taught the chick how to not get scared when the bear comes and then the girl was no longer worried about the chick at night. The chick was also happy now because she wasn't scared of the bear!

Isabelle Mannion (10)

Junction Farm Primary School, Eaglescliffe

Kindstar With A New Friend

Kindstar was lonely in the loud park. Suddenly, Kindstar had to go to a new, important school. Kindstar was very worried.

"I wish I had friends," said Kindstar. In a busy crowd at school, Kindstar was looking for a friend. Kindstar was kind-hearted but everyone was mean. After that, there was a kind boy called Eyow. Eyow came up slowly to Kindstar and said, "You haven't checked our classroom." And then Eyow was Kindstar's first friend in the whole entire world!

Yafa Abuzaid (7)
Junction Farm Primary School, Eaglescliffe

Bobsled's Olympic Adventure!

Once upon a time, a cheeky little green monster called Bobsled went to The Winter Olympics. He went to the Olympics to take part in the skeleton run. He was not very good at the skeleton run because he always banged his head! On the morning of the competition, he was very excited and got up early to watch the sunrise and it made him feel good. He went to the top of the track, got on his sled and pushed off. Bob went super duper fast and didn't bang his head. Bob came first and was happy!

Kayne Bibby (7)
Junction Farm Primary School, Eaglescliffe

Monsters Are My Friends

Don't be afraid, he hides under my bed and in my secret wardrobe tunnel. When no one is around, he pops out and likes to jump on my bed, play hide-and-seek and play my drums. We laugh a lot.
He's big, blue, green and fluffy. He's so squidgy, I just love to squeeze him. I ride on his back and he keeps me safe. So don't be afraid, be brave and strong. That's why monsters are my friends. Don't be afraid, I'm never alone. Hugbert is always by my side.

Zacharia Kabir (7)
Junction Farm Primary School, Eaglescliffe

36

A Bad Monster

Once upon a time, there was a little monster called Jerdle and he was a mean monster who pushes people and his friends. He went into the forest and saw a cottage and saw a bit of smoke coming from the chimney and smelt some bread. He went into the home and saw a monster cooking food and went back home and told his mum all about it, all of it and went to bed. Night night.

Rubie Loredo (6)

Junction Farm Primary School, Eaglescliffe

Monster Goes To Birthday Party Park

Once upon a time lived a monster that was going to a birthday party and ate a lot of cake, sweets, chocolate chip cookies and cupcakes. Then he was full up so he went to sleep and when he woke up, then everyone was gone so he goes to the park and played. Then he saw his friends then they played again. Then they all went home.

Mason Clark (5)

Junction Farm Primary School, Eaglescliffe

Bobly And The Sandy Beach

Once upon a time, there was a monster called Bobly. He was five years old. He went to the busy swimming pool which was huge and he got very wet. Then he got home and told his parents that he was really wet. Then he went to the sandy beach and it was busy. He had to wait in a busy queue then he lived happily ever after.

Inaaya Riaz (7)

Junction Farm Primary School, Eaglescliffe

Bob's Beach Adventure

My monster is at a beach. It is lovely. I saw crabs, he saw a spiky, bumpy and creepy crab. I need sun cream so I don't get burnt. The sun cream felt weird. But I liked it. The monster made sandcastles. We made a moat. We joined it to the sea. The sea was cold. We ended the day with a barbecue.

Joshua Horseman (6)
Junction Farm Primary School, Eaglescliffe

Doughnuts With Chocolate

In a faraway Dunkin' Donuts, a doughnut escaped. He was a stealer of doughnuts. He had found Chocolatina, who went missing ages ago. But then, "Ahh!" Chocolatina sprayed Donehut and ran. Donehut was sad, he cried sprinkles and he made a friend out of sprinkles. But then Chocolatina, the monster, came back and exclaimed, "You will never stop me!"

"Oh yes, we will," Donehut replied. The sprinkle monster started crying more sprinkles. Donehut was trying to defend, but then a real person picked Chocolatina up and used her. The monster was gone!

"We are free. No more bad guys!"

Joshua Groves (10)
Listerdale Junior Academy, Brecks

Tiny Tim And His Enemy

This is Tiny-Tim, the GOAT of football. When Tim was young, he practised football 24/7 which is why he is amazing. His enemy, Big-Bob, was so strong, he could take down everyone. This Saturday, the two had a game and were prepared.

"It's finally the big day!" announced the commentator. The couple met at halfway point. Tiny's team got the kick.

"It's the last kick of the game," said the commentator. "And Tiny has the ball. Ohh, what a goal by Tiny-Tim. He has won Tiny-Town the game and beat his rival's team!" Tiny-Titans were celebrating. The Big-Bandits were not.

Bella Downey (10)
Listerdale Junior Academy, Brecks

We Are Here For Each Other

Cuddles is a cat from Planet Unique. She was wondering what would happen if she went to Earth. She asked her parents.

"Can I go to Earth?" she screamed as loud as an eagle.

"You will not go to Earth! Do you understand?"

"Yes," she gulped. "Great! *Now I am busted for life. I don't care.*" She hopped out of her bed. "I am *going!*" She limped to the spaceship. She landed on Earth. "*Wait, we are here.*" As soon as she walked, people laughed at her and tried to hurt her. What do you think will happen next?

Zara Qamran (11)
Listerdale Junior Academy, Brecks

The Golden Refugee

The night it happened, the country was struck with great force. A war began! A monster, no younger than nine, forever out of his home, left to fend for himself! The cries were so loud they could tear the sky. The country, taken hostage. Since the war started, the monster now known as Crier Tonaldo came to Britain. He started his football career at Sporting, going on to play for Real Madrid, Manchester United and Juventus! Winning the Ballon d'Or and UCLs, he brought himself and Portugal back to their feet. Finding himself and the game of football saved him.

Elliott Brown (11)
Listerdale Junior Academy, Brecks

Is There A Monster Under My Bed?!

When I was younger I'd hear strange noises coming from under my bed! I believed there was a monster... There was! It started when one night, I took it into my own hands. I peered under my bed, yet before I could scream, the monster-like creature said, "Hi, I'm Gertrude. I promise I won't hurt you with my sharps rows of teeth!" I was scared at first and was going to yelp and scream help! Ever since then we've been inseparable, even my family loves her. That just goes to show, not all monsters are mean, cold-hearted creatures at all.

Eliza Rudram (11)

Listerdale Junior Academy, Brecks

Tiny-Teeny

Tiny-Teeny is a little monster. He goes to a school for monsters. He is the only monster with no legs. When he wants to move, his arms stretch. The bigger monsters ask Tiny-Teeny to race, just to put him under pressure because they know they'll win. The older monsters leave primary to go to a monster camp. Finally, Tiny-Teeny can have a rest from being bullied all the time. Tiny-Teeny has three years with no bullying. Now it's his time to leave school. He ends up getting into the same school as the other, older monsters. He is scared.

Eliza Briggs (11)
Listerdale Junior Academy, Brecks

The Attacker Zombie

Here it was, the first-ever person to be brought back to life. Celebrating his achievement, John started to hear strange noises. Looking down, he saw that Zach had his eyes wide open but they looked like swirls. His face started to become misshapen and horrible, turning into some sort of monster. Standing up, the monster started chasing John, trying to convince him to stop running. Without thinking, he obeyed Zach and stopped running. He started yelling at John, asking him why he didn't leave him in peace. John was never seen again.

Amelia Sherwood (10)

Listerdale Junior Academy, Brecks

Coco And The Mystery Treasure Hunt

Coco and Chloe were gardening and saw a shiny box. She opened it and found a treasure map. Chloe pointed her tail to the directions. They came across a human village. Coco got scared. Chloe turned into a bat and took them over the village and carried on with her journey, walking for miles. Then she came across a cave. She walked in and found a trap so she crawled across. Coco got extremely hungry and got food out of her small bag. She shared it with Chloe, then found a treasure chest and a creepy old man. "It's Grandad!"

Evie Shelton (10)

Listerdale Junior Academy, Brecks

Spiralz's Lost Daughter

Spiralz works at Monster Topia, a place where there's sea life and where you can stay for as long as you like at Monster Topia's Hotel. Spiralz's role is to make sure people have a good time at the park. One morning, whilst he was getting his suit and tie on, he noticed his two-year-old daughter Tarpee had gone missing. He checked the wardrobe and under the bed. All he found were two monsters. They weren't very nice. Suddenly, he got a phone call from his boss saying his daughter was found swimming with the animals.

Elizah Zia (11)

Listerdale Junior Academy, Brecks

The Travel To Human World

Once there was a monster called Goggles. She was so wild and free with a best friend until... they went to the human world. As she got off her boat, she couldn't believe her eyes. As she walked to a place called Medowall, everyone screamed with fear and was about to call the police. A few seconds later, the police arrived with guns and armour thinking she was some kind of animal. They screamed, "Hands up!" as they grabbed her tightly. She tried to run but they chucked her into a cage and took her somewhere unknown...

Lexi Sayles (11)

Listerdale Junior Academy, Brecks

Monster Tragedy

There was a boy named Henry and he made the worst mistake of his life. You're probably wondering what his mistake was... Let me just say he opened the gates to monsters. Yeah, monsters! Here's Henry's story. He was once on a walk when he suddenly ran into a gate. He decided to go inside and as soon as he did, he walked straight into a monster, Stanley! Henry raced out of there when he noticed that whilst he was getting chased, Stanley was crushing houses. So Henry made a smart turn around and led him into the gates!

Ellie Draycott (11)
Listerdale Junior Academy, Brecks

The Legendary Concert

Dedicated to the Foo Fighters

Once Rolly the Rocker wanted to get concert tickets. He bought them and on his way, he faced a problem. Tibby the Terrible was trying to cancel the concert, guarding it and hissing at everybody! So Rolly confronted him and they got into an argument! The band heard him and Dave the rock god with his powerful guitar blew Tibby away with his powerful music and energy. Tibby was gone, never to be seen or heard of again. Then Rolly and everyone else got to the concert for free in celebration of the defeat of Tibby the Terrible.

Jazzy Lewis (11)

Listerdale Junior Academy, Brecks

The Mystery Of Blobby

There once was a boy called Blobby. He went missing at the age of ten. What nobody knew was that his sister shrunk him with his dad's shrink ray. After, she squirmed out with a smug grin and was never to be seen again. Until one day, whilst his mum was dusting, she thought she saw something. She examined it closer and it was Blobby wearing a top hat. She was frozen in shock, but then she reached down and grabbed him. Then she gave him the biggest hug ever. That day, they threw the biggest welcoming party ever.

Joseph Sharp (11)
Listerdale Junior Academy, Brecks

Wiggles Saves The Day!

Wiggles is one of the cutest monsters you'll ever see, but when she sees a duck, she goes mental. This is because a few years ago, Planet Duck invaded Planet Monster. So because Wiggles was angry, she face-planted into a pond and got a mouthful of pond water and it tasted gross! So then she had the idea to get her water gun and load it with pond water and fire it at them. The ducks hated it and thought it was gross too! So they ran away. After that, Planet Monster was happy forever. They love their pond water!

Edith Roebuck (10)
Listerdale Junior Academy, Brecks

The Time Alter

Have you ever wondered who controls the time? Well, that'll be the time twins. One bad, one good. These mischievous monsters live in separate places. Lumo lives at the top of Big Ben and Luma the bad time warper, lives in the core of the Earth. One night, Lumo saw a mysterious figure lurking in the shadows. It was Luma. Upon this time, they didn't know they were twins. He came to defeat Lumo. They started to brawl until half of a ripped picture fell out of each of the twin's pockets. They matched!

Harvey Elliott (11)

Listerdale Junior Academy, Brecks

Friends Forever

Chewey and Stuff are best friends. When they got older, Stuff left and went to live in France. Four years later, Chewey was missing Stuff so he decided to go and find his friend. So he set off on his way. First, he came to a bridge but the bridge started to break so Chewey ran across and just made it in time. A few hours later, he came to a cave. A dark cave. He entered the cave at a run. After miles of running, he finally saw some light. He was there! The friends are reunited once more.

Emily Smith (10)
Listerdale Junior Academy, Brecks

Eggy

Eggy has a little brother and they are kept in a storage room at Morrisons. Eggy tries to crack his little brother. On the eighth day, a big monster comes to buy Eggy but decides not to. When they go on the shelves, Eggy gets annoyed and tries to push his little brother off the shelf. A monster comes to buy Eggy. Someone then comes to buy his little brother. When they get home, they paint and keep him forever. His new family takes great care of him. He loves it!

Ellie-Mae Hastie (11)

Listerdale Junior Academy, Brecks

A Monster In A Lost World

One quiet evening, Ferned felt ravenous, more ravenous than ever. The shivering trees hid from the anger Ferned was holding. Suddenly, another monster appeared. Ferned felt a sense of regret returning to these horrid woods. With precision, Ferned carefully got the monster's ability and all the other abilities he'd stolen. Ferned's tentacle legs were shaking fiercely until one moment, it all ended. His powers, his hope, his everything! He collapsed, in reality, he was nothing. He was evil, malicious, mischievous, all the words you can think of. His whole life was gone and no one could do anything about it!

Leon Vandra-Simon (11)
Lockers Park School, Hemel Hempstead

Squishie The Town Hero

Squishie was a harmless but disgusting monster. No one liked him. Then in his postbox, he had a letter. Mythical monsters were on the way to destroy his town. Everyone started to panic but Squishie was brave and prepared for battle. He could splutter toxic stuff as his superpower. Then mythical monsters arrived. They started to destroy the town. Squishie had a plan. He was jumping into monsters' mouths and spluttering toxic stuff. It made holes in monsters and they understood that they best be friends with Squishie. That's how Squishie saved the town and became Town Hero.

German Pankov (11)

Lockers Park School, Hemel Hempstead

Cooler And His Loneliness

A long time ago in Bonk City lived Cooler and his sister, Mooler. As every other monster had a power, Cooler's one was to turn cool whilst Mooler's was coloured emotions. One day, Cooler walked into the town square and suddenly everyone loved him! Everything was free for him, VIP passes and even new cars! One night, after days of pleasure, he was asked to do a speech on the main stage! "This is amazing!" After the speech, he was number one popular which was too popular. So when he got home he said, "Sorry," and hugged his sad sister.

Andrey Pavlov (10)
Lockers Park School, Hemel Hempstead

Fwea's Journey

Once upon a time, when mystical monsters still ruled Earth, Fwea was the legend that they still told. The story was passed down through generations and over time, the story became exaggerated. So today, I am telling you the true story of Fwea... One day, at the very beginning of time, Fwea was unleashed to create the Earth. He was made of fire, water, earth, and air. He set out on his mission to create Earth. He summoned a mythical dragon to help him. They worked day and night then after three glorphnorps (four years), they finally completed their quest.

Matthew Lewis (10)

Lockers Park School, Hemel Hempstead

Rollers' Journey

Once upon a time, there was a monster called Rollers. He lived in Spike City. He could crush anything and climb anything. But he had an enemy, Hopston. Hopston was planning to burn down a defenceless old woman's house with his rocket boots so Rollers had to quickly eat his breakfast. *Chomp, chomp.* He ate his breakfast and set off on his journey to Spike City centre. He took the tube. While he was on the tube, everyone cheered him on, awaiting his big battle. Once he left, he saw Hopston. Just in time, he smashed his boots and won.

Jonathan Elia (10)
Lockers Park School, Hemel Hempstead

Scrappy And The Terrible Housekeeping

One day Scrappy came from his lair and found that there was a house above his lair. He ate his way through the floor of the house and made a home in the basement of doom. The next day, a boy wanted to get his football from the basement but he smelt a pungent smell and ran away. Scrappy stayed as it was his home. The boy went to go tell his parents to get him out of there. The boy's parents came down to the basement to get Scrappy out. Scrappy left out of the door and lived healthily.

Thomas Pinchin (10)

Lockers Park School, Hemel Hempstead

Monara The Living Toy

Nina had gotten presents for Christmas. But she got a very special present, Monara! As Nina went to sleep, she heard a chuckle.

"Ahh!" she screamed.

"Are you okay?" Monara asked.

"Umm, who are you?" Nina asked.

"I'm Monara, a bonkers monster. Let's be friends!"

"Yes!" Nina screamed. "But there is one problem, my mum!" she shouted.

"What about her?" Monara questioned.

"She doesn't know about you," Nina said.

"Then let's tell her!" Monara exclaimed. And they went into the kitchen to tell Nina's mum and... she was fine with it! So they became one happy family.

Teni Bamigboye (9)

Macaulay CE Primary School, Clapham

Hannah Meets Spine

Hannah was in her bedroom when she saw something move under her bed. It was a monster! The monster was purple and spiny, like a hedgehog with hazel eyes.

"Hello," said the monster. It had a croaky voice. "My name is Spine."

"I'm Hannah," said Hannah. Spine explained that she had been going to her cousin, Spike's, birthday party on the moon when her ship broke down. She said that if she was quick, she might make it to the lunar disco.

"My mum works at NASA," explained Hannah. "You can use one of the rockets there." So Spine did.

Imogen Kempsey (9)
Macaulay CE Primary School, Clapham

Lulu's Earth Adventure

One day Lulu was bored when she found something to do! Lulu decided to take a spin around the solar system when there was a meteorite coming toward her! *Boom!* Suddenly, she was on a different planet called Earth! A little girl ran towards her and picked her up to take her inside.

"What am I doing here?" said Lulu.

"Your ship crashed," said the girl.

How am I going to get home? wondered Lulu. Lulu found out what she had to do. She asked the girl for some milk, mustard, oil, crumbs and sweets and then she flew back.

Ava Toemehn (9)

Macaulay CE Primary School, Clapham

Hero Stops Climate Change

Hero watched the sun melting his home. He was a polar bear and the hot weather made him angry. People were polluting his home, causing climate change. All the bears were suffering. Hero put on his cape and went to see Princess Crystal and King Kevin, to get them to stop people polluting the ocean, the Arctic and chopping down forests. They also had to stop them from using oil. So they did. King Kevin cleaned up the sea and Crystal planted trees. Hero went home and told everyone what happened and had some fish fingers for tea with ketchup.

Milly Andrews (9)

Macaulay CE Primary School, Clapham

Mountain Jail

Deep in the mountains of Monsterville lived a delightful monster called Funny Legs and as you can probably guess, he had a lot of legs! He had a big enemy, King Greenie Weenie of the Flies. When Funny Legs was taking a stroll around the mountains, he saw King Greenie Weenie! The King flew down, as he was a fly, and said that he owned the mountains but Funny Legs said that he owned the mountains as he lived there. They started getting really cross with each other but in the end, Funny Legs had the King locked up forever.

Lola Hodges (9)

Macaulay CE Primary School, Clapham

Cookie's Adventure

Wishes can come true. Cookie goes to the forest to get mangos. When she gets there, she finds lots of yummy mangos, but Cookie hears rustling in the bushes. It's a tiger! Cookie wants to run but doesn't want to drop a mango. The tiger chases her. Cookie runs, throwing five mangos for the tiger to eat. The tiger thanks Cookie and they become friends. Every day, Cookie comes and gets mangos for the tiger and meets a friend on the way. Cookie gets more mangos to share every day to eat with her friends and family.

Brooklyn Harper (8)

Macaulay CE Primary School, Clapham

Wishes Can Come True

Wishes can come true. I find they happen when you least expect. Is it the same for you? Well, my story is about something I did, that I thought was impossible. So read on. When I was a little Sowolina on the planet Zondo, I wanted to win a swimming race, except water terrified me. On the day of the race, my teachers tried, but I was not prepared. Then, just as the race was beginning, an asteroid crashed nearby! I dived into the pool, fearlessly swimming two lengths. I won my race! Isn't that amazing?

Theo Swash (9)

Macaulay CE Primary School, Clapham

Cheeto, The Bed Monster

Once a girl found something under her bed. She was anxious about what it could be. It was a monster. She wanted to help it. Together their friendship would never end. One day, they found a portal. The monster said this would take him home. And from that day on, Cheeto was never seen again.

Eve Reid (8)

Macaulay CE Primary School, Clapham

Golgm's Adventure!

Ellie is getting a glass of water when she sees Golgm standing there. He wants to get home but he needs rubbish to power his engine. Ellie runs to get lots of rubbish. Once full of power, she waves her new friend goodbye and he promises to visit.

Eleanor Whittle (9)

Macaulay CE Primary School, Clapham

The Scared Monster

Once upon a time, there was a monster called Scared Monster. This monster had very sharp teeth and twenty eyes but he was very shy to show them. He was purple. He lived in Scotland. He had the power to fly. One day, a girl came by and saw Scared Monster. He lived in a shed. Scared Monster loves art. But when the girl passed, she saw Scared Monster. She loved monsters. She took him to school. He loved it so everyone called him Happy Monster from then on.

Amelie Nisbet (6)
Mossend Primary School, Bellshill

Wither Storm's Stages

My monster's name is Wither Storm. It has six stages. The first stage is not so bad. In the second stage it... starts to protect itself. Third, it grows a tentacle. The fourth stage, it grows giant. Fifth, more giant and it gets three big heads and ten or six tentacles. Sixth, it has a big brain.

Finnlay Nisbet (6)
Mossend Primary School, Bellshill

Izzy The Bonkers Monster

Hi, I'm Izzy and I'm a Bonkers Monster. I travel all over the world. Today, I found where I'm going to stop. It's at my friend Caoimhe's because we met at school.

Caoimhe Rooney (7)
Mossend Primary School, Bellshill

Monsters

My monster's name is Crazy Lazy. My monster has three pets. A rabbit, a dog and a monster hamster. My monster likes to sleep on Mondays. My monster likes to party on Fridays.

Ellie Mullin (7)

Mossend Primary School, Bellshill

Judy's First Time At Zootropolis

My monster is called Judy. She lives in Zootropolis. My monster can talk to animals. My monster is nice. My monster has a wolf as a pet. The wolf is called Lally.

Olivia van den Berg (6)

Mossend Primary School, Bellshill

Monster Village

My monster is called Friday. My monster lives in a penguin. The penguin ate him. My monster's power is that he can swim. He can eat sweets and he has a pet.

Isla Mae Currie (7)
Mossend Primary School, Bellshill

Bananas Monster

My monster is called Banapoo. My monster lives in Africa. My monster has a pet banana. My monster can breathe bananas.

Isla Liddell (5)

Mossend Primary School, Bellshill

Jumping Monster

My monster is called Sun of Moon. My monster lives underground. My monster can jump high into a ball pit.

Taylor Campbell (5)
Mossend Primary School, Bellshill

Monster Dodo's Happy Birthday!

One day it was Dodo's birthday, she thought she would go to the park after breakfast.

"Oh!" she shouted. "I forgot I have art class, then I can go to the park."

At the park, her friends surprised her with a party. They played games, danced and had a picnic with chocolate croissants and strawberry milkshakes. Next, they went to the seaside to play on the sandy beach. They found a secret tunnel which led them to a hidden treasure chest with a heavenly chocolate and strawberry cake inside.

"Suprise!" her friends shouted.

Dodo replied, "Thank you. Best birthday ever!"

Faith Vaja (6)

St Joseph's Catholic Primary School, Northfleet

The Half Demon

"Oh no!" cried the angel. "Half of my body has fallen into the realms of the forbidden land!" What did this mean? Half of the angel's body had turned into a demon! Anxious, the half-demon flew swiftly towards the village, hoping to find a way to return to the bright, friendly angel he once was. Instead, his fears came true. He attacked the village, causing spikes to rise from the ground, creating panic. Suddenly, remembering the portal, the half-demon soared towards it, knowing that once inside his chance to be a full angel would come again. He hoped!

Elliot Hodge (9)

St Joseph's Catholic Primary School, Northfleet

The Saviour Of America

One day TT was living her ordinary life. She went to school but TT's desire was to be homeschooled because every day, Bonkers came up to her and bullied her. TT cheered up by singing a song called 'The sun will come out tomorrow'. One ordinary Friday morning, the news reporter said in a serious voice that a witch was bringing segregation back from history. The witch was on TT's road so TT ran outside.

"This is not Atlanta, this is Nigeria," she said.

"Here," TT said. But TT grabbed the witch and took it to jail.

Temilayo Adesina (8)

St Joseph's Catholic Primary School, Northfleet

Sprout's Lucky Day!

Sprout woke up on a sunny Sunday. He rushed downstairs to check if there was any post. There it was, a card waiting for him at the doorstep. Sprout ripped it open with his sharp claws. Inside he found his first ever library card. Yipee!

He brushed his hair and charged out the door to the library. In the library Sprout found his favourite book, *'Fantastic Hairdressers for Monsters'*. It had a bright green cover with mega monster hairstyles. Sprout couldn't wait to show his friends at monster school. It really was his lucky day!

Emily Chama (7)
St Joseph's Catholic Primary School, Northfleet

The Break-Up

Once upon a time, there was a little monster girl called Macky. She was very grateful, kind and generous until she moved into Year 5. Her classmates suddenly became unkind and mean towards her. They would bully her, tell lies and make up stories to get Macky in trouble. She was devastated and in shock. But, the meaner they were, the nicer Macky was to them.

Macky was later blessed with a lovely new friend called Allie. They soon became BFFs and would spend most of their time together. Her old friends' bad attitude did not matter any more.

Maryam Sassou (9)

St Joseph's Catholic Primary School, Northfleet

Bouncy's Football Day

Bouncy was feeling lonely because all of his friends were afraid of him because he looked scary. He was tall and covered in blue hair with orange googly eyes. Also he had really sharp teeth and bounced a lot. So nobody played with him. So one day, he joined a football club. His teammates couldn't believe how fast he was on the pitch. They hadn't won so many games before. Bouncy was so proud of himself. He showed people that he wasn't scary. He was so popular. So he said, "I finally found me some friends!" He was so happy.

Mikie Brown-Deane (7)
St Joseph's Catholic Primary School, Northfleet

Cry Baby Eater

Once upon a time, there was an inactive, sobbing monster called Cry Baby Eater. He had baby blue fur, one gigantic eye in the middle of his face and the roundest, stubbiest teeth. He lived in Monster World and attended Monster Primary School. He was utterly greedy and never did his work. Although his favourite lesson was maths, art was his least preferred one. One day, his first lesson of the day, art. He exceedingly hated it but that was not the problem. The problem was that he had to draw a human though he had never seen one before...

Kyra Manan (8)

St Joseph's Catholic Primary School, Northfleet

Monkers' Day At The Park

One morning, a little monster named Monkers woke up. He stretched and got up. He had breakfast but then thought, *now today I'll go to the park and have a picnic for breakfast*. Today was a very special day so he had his favourite pancakes. After breakfast, he brushed his teeth, got his picnic basket and headed to the park. At the park, he laid his blanket on the grass. He set it up. He wasn't hungry yet so he played on the swing then he got hungry so he had some tea, sandwiches and chocolate. After, he went home.

Annie Bennett (7)
St Joseph's Catholic Primary School, Northfleet

Polkadots Vs Stripes, Friends Vs Friends

Once there was a happy planet, Dotty Planet. Everyone is all friends and they live a happy life. One day, monsters from another planet invade. Freckles, known as the expert at making friends, tries to stop them but The Stripes wouldn't listen. Freckles says a speech to all of them until they listen. The Stripes realise you should always be kind. The Stripes go to their planet and find out their planet is destroyed! Freckles says, "Come live with us!" So now they're all friends of Dotty and Stripy Planet.

Tilly Byrne (10)

St Joseph's Catholic Primary School, Northfleet

Roco Fears

Upon a lonely mountain lived a monster, a nice monster called Roco. You see Roco didn't have friends. Since, well, he thought humans were bad but that all changed one day when Roco went to a lake for a walk and he saw humans coming his way. He hid behind a skinny tree in the hope they wouldn't see him, but you see, Roco wasn't the smallest monster. They saw him. Roco closed his eyes and put his hands over his ears, thinking they'd scream, but they didn't. They invited him to their picnic, so he did.

Ethne Scullion-Smith (11)

St Joseph's Catholic Primary School, Northfleet

Big Monster

Once upon a time, there was a girl called Alice who lived with her parents. Alice's mum told her not to go outside at night but she did. When Alice was returning home, she met a monster and ran.

The monster said, "Where did you go?"

"To a friend," said Alice.

The monster replied, "I am going to eat you!" She ran to the house but the gate was locked. She called Mum and Dad to open the door, but they didn't let her in and the monster ate her up.

Jayden Kyle Botwe (6)

St Joseph's Catholic Primary School, Northfleet

The Upla Dupla

On a shiny moon, there was an alien called Upla Dupla and he lived on the moon. One night Upla Dupla fell off the moon, into a space train and travelled to Australia. He walked and walked until the morning when he saw a kangaroo. They bounced to London and met the Queen in Buckingham Palace. They asked the Queen to help Upla Dupla. The Queen was so kind to agree. After Upla Dupla reached his home, he sent a thank you letter to the Queen. The Queen was very happy to read the letter.

Raiya Nair (6)
St Joseph's Catholic Primary School, Northfleet

A Monster Called Thunder

Once upon a time, in a village called Flowerville was born a cute, fluffy baby monster. He was different from the others. When Thunder, that's his name, started nursery, everyone was afraid of him. Nobody wanted to play with him. One day, a cat from the nursery climbed up into a tree. Only brave Thunder helped the cat to come down. Since then all the children found out that although Thunder looks scary, he has a big heart. You can't judge someone by their appearance.

Sophie Wisniewska (7)

St Joseph's Catholic Primary School, Northfleet

The Friendless Monster

In the morning Grinchette woke up early because she wanted to try and make friends in the human world. She went to the portal that led to the human world and then she asked everyone but they were scared. When she came back, she was sad because she did not make any friends, but then she had an idea! She could try to make friends in her village and she did. Her friend's name was Sandy because she loved the sand. Next, they went into the forge to get best friend necklaces.

Anaiya Rodriques (7)
St Joseph's Catholic Primary School, Northfleet

Blob The Monster Saves The Day

Blob the monster was hairy, people found him quite scary. Blob the monster was boring. He became braver one morning. Blob heard someone screaming loud, it even attracted a crowd. He felt big and brave. Blob gleefully saved the day. He quickly ran straight outside. The crown unhappily sighed. Blob the monster didn't cave, he got ready and prepared. A cat was in a tree, so Blob set it free. Everyone in the crowd cheered. And then Blob suddenly disappeared.

India Keeble (11)

St Joseph's Catholic Primary School, Northfleet

Snowbomb Goes To Mars

Snowbomb travelled from Pluto to Mars in a snow rocket. It melted after landing. She realised it was very hot. Snowbomb was feeling sad and lonely. Then she saw a volcano and wanted to explore it. Inside the volcano, she found an alien named Flame. They soon became friends and BFFs. Flame showed Snowbomb his home. Snowbomb missed home and pointed at Pluto. Flame wanted Snowbomb to be happy and gave her his rocket. Snowbomb waved goodbye and went back home.

Tayla Mark-Ihama (7)
St Joseph's Catholic Primary School, Northfleet

Izzy Finding Friends

Once upon a time, Izzy, the bonkers monster, went to find her friends but she couldn't find them at all. She looked everywhere, including the park which her friends loved. She peeked into a shipwreck and found them guarded by sharks. She had to make a plan. Izzy distracted the sharks and her friends got away. Izzy escaped through a small hole that was too small for the sharks. Izzy and her friends went to the cinema because Izzy did a good job.

Ruby Timlin (6)
St Joseph's Catholic Primary School, Northfleet

Zagner's Best Match

On Sunday, when Zagner woke up, he was very excited about his league trophy. After breakfast, he rode his car to his stadium called Danger Place. When the game started, he scored the first goal in ten minutes. After half-time, in the fiftieth minute, Zagner scored a penalty! His celebration was a knee slide. The match ended 4-2 and Zagner and his friends won the League Trophy. When he was home, he was very proud of himself and his team.

Jeremy Pulik (7)
St Joseph's Catholic Primary School, Northfleet

Frozemole The Hero

Frozemole lived a happy life and was well-fed because of all the yummy ground food. But one day, Mole went everywhere and froze up the ground. Suddenly, all the ground food was gone. It was cold. Mole knew what he had to do, so he caught the sun! Mole ran back to the ground and let the sun out! All the ground food came back and he feasted greatly all day long. Yum!

Iris Rea (8)

St Joseph's Catholic Primary School, Northfleet

Count Joker's Friend

It all started at 10am. He was in school with his friends Clowning Pie and Smelly. He invited his twenty-eight friends except for Serious Wealthy. He always gets Fs for not playing jokes and pranks. So he still came with his headphones to read 99,999 books, and when he was on his 36,549 book, Joker bit him for two minutes. Warning, beware of Count Joker.

Eitan Adekunle-Adebayo (7)
St Joseph's Catholic Primary School, Northfleet

Rainbow Glitter

I had a Bonkers Monster called Rainbow Glitter and we went to a party and we made some slime. After that, we went to the shop and we bought some milk, apples and bananas and then we went home. When we were at home, we played video games. After that, we went to bed.

Kehinde Adekunle (6)
St Joseph's Catholic Primary School, Northfleet

The Battle

Once, a good monster, Acry, who was super acrobatic and could grow extra limbs, was trying to track down a bad guy, Cactus Man. Acry travelled through the place where she was born, a huge jungle, China, the pacific and at Lego Land and cartwheeled through everything. Then she saw him, Cactus Man.

"How about a little fight?" sneered Cactus Man. "Sure," smiled Acry. Acry quickly grew eight more limbs. The battle lasted three nights. Literally, they just kicked each other. Then Cactus Man started crying and wept, "I'll be good!"

Next, Acry said, "Okay!" After that they became friends.

Evie Connell (8)

Three Bridges Primary School, Three Bridges

Dorito Overcomes His Fear

One day, Dorito, a bonkers monster, was walking cheerfully through Broccoli Forest in Food Land while he walked back home to Mount Chip. When he got home he saw a letter. It said: 'Someone else is going to move into Mount Chip'.

"What? But-but I can't leave my home! Aargh!" He started going crazy.

The next day, he went to talk to Pizza. "Pizza, I need your help!"

"Are you leaving Mount Chip?"

"Yes!"

"Okay, your new home could be better!"

"Really?"

"Yes!"

When Dorito left Mount Chip he did have a better home.

Abdullah Umair (7)
Three Bridges Primary School, Three Bridges

Zankyra

There was a monster called Zankyfra. He wasn't a scary monster. His mum said, "You might be when you grow up."

"Your mum's right. Zankyfra, do you want to go to the surface?"

"Yes please, Dad."

"So if you want to be a scary monster you have to be scary."

"How do I get scary though?"

"Do you have any tricks?"

"Yeah, I can climb and do backflips."

"So let's climb on that building. Put this mask on and climb."

"Aargh! Why are there tiny monsters in my house?! Mummy, help me!"

Harvey Kelsey (8)
Three Bridges Primary School, Three Bridges

Herobrine Vs Monster Exebrine

Boss Creeper hoped for a new monster so got an egg and kept it until Sunday. At 12pm on Sunday, the egg hatched. Boss Creeper named the monster Monster Exebrine. Boss Creeper told it to attack the world.

Herobrine, Herobrine Girl, Hero and Haikbrine were training. XDJames and Monster Crafters and Herobrine were playing Herobrine's PS6. They played Herocraft. Exebrine exploded Sumiyah's house. The Herobrines stopped playing the PS6. K2BE came to help his brothers fight Monster Exbrine. XDBrineStudio2 came too. They captured them. K2BE ran. He got a gun and sent the monster to prison. Everyone was scared.

Ogooluwa Folami (7)

Three Bridges Primary School, Three Bridges

The Monster Who Loved To Help Too Much

Gzolydovelove was a good person with a great job. But, the problem was that she could not stop helping people, and you would think that was a good thing, but when she helped people, she got distracted.

One morning, her boss shouted, "If you don't focus, I will take further action." That day in the pet shop, Gzolydovelove cried and cried, when suddenly, Maddiefood, her enemy, walked in.

"Listen, I know what happened, so just take my advice."

Gzoly did take Maddiefood's advice and believe it or not, it worked. Whenever she wanted to help, she distracted herself with work.

Aishani Chowdhuri (9)

Three Bridges Primary School, Three Bridges

The Story Of Lolly Sprinkle

One morning in the village Icicle was a monster, Lolly Sprinkle. It was the most joyful place. Lolly had the cutest powers, she could shoot out ice cream. There was one problem. Chocolate Flake was the meanest of all. Everyone was afraid of her, except for Lolly. "I will put an end to this meanness." It was enough.

Later that day, she saw Chocolate Flake was being mean because she didn't have enough friends. She felt sad. She needed friends, everyone needs some friends. She went to her and said, "I will be your friend, you just need training."

Ishana Verma (7)

Three Bridges Primary School, Three Bridges

The Clumsy Balloon That Learnt To Be Brave

One year ago, there was a balloon and her name was Miss Clumsy. She was one of the clumsiest balloons. Every day, she had to see her enemy, Stormy. She was a lightning-shaped balloon. One day, she saw Stormy. Stormy flew to Miss Clumsy, then Stormy started a fight. But, just then, the headteacher Mrs Noormohammad came. She said madly, "Both of you come to my office now!" They went. The headteacher only told off Miss Clumsy. Then, Miss Clumsy explained and the headteacher understood. She told Stormy that she would miss her play. From then, Miss Clumsy was brave.

Anjana Theepan (8)
Three Bridges Primary School, Three Bridges

Sneaky And His Sister

Sneaky was hiding in a tree so he didn't have to fight with his sister because they got into an argument. They got into an argument because he got the same toy as his sister's toy. So he got into an argument and said, "Take yours back!"
"No, take yours back!" They went on and on, they never stopped arguing.
So Sneaky told his mum and she said, "Take both toys back."
So Sneaky and his sister put both the toys back and they got different toys and they were happy and didn't argue and they became best friends forever.

Alex Emmans (8)
Three Bridges Primary School, Three Bridges

Kooper's Team

Kooper the monster was good at getting a team. Kooper's quest was to fight bad guys. Soon he found a bad guy. Luckily, he had a sword with him. Somehow Kooper won. After Kooper won a monster came up to him and said, "Can I join your team for fighting?"

Kooper said, "Yes!" So they travelled before a monster appeared and another monster said the same thing. "Okay!" said Kooper.

Suddenly, all the monsters came out at once and the team won. Once they fought them they went to Kooper's house to have a party. They were so happy.

Joshua Callaghan (8)
Three Bridges Primary School, Three Bridges

The Twin Battlers

On Mars one day, someone called Dwanjonson woke up and met someone called Cookie. Dwanjonson got his katana and Cookie got his ninja stars. They wanted to see who was the strongest and the best battler. They had many, many battles and Cookie found out they were famous twins. So they had one more battle. It was crazy. Dwanjonson cut Cookie's arm off then Cookie cut off Dwanjonson's hand so Dwanjonson called for World War Three with aircraft, battle buses and tanks. The world turned dark. Every day, they would bomb people and he stopped World War Three.

Ricky-Lee
Three Bridges Primary School, Three Bridges

The Story Of Tricky

Tricky's a monster who does tricks like skateboarding, roller skating and any other things. Tricky also likes to pranking people. Tricky went to school and all the people there made fun of him because he had a green tongue and yellow teeth. One day at home, he was so sad that he spent hours brushing his teeth. He finally got his teeth white clean. Then he did a backflip to celebrate his white teeth and knocked the tap off. His mum was coming up the stairs and shouted, "What was all that racket?"
Was this one of Tricky's pranks?

Alice Larkins (8)
Three Bridges Primary School, Three Bridges

Baseball Billy

One time, in Fireball Town, there was the best basketballer in the whole universe. He fought crime and once there was an evil mastermind named Baseball Billy, Baller Jr's arch-nemesis. Baller Jr found him and they fought each other. Baller got the first strike. The first was one of his best attacks, hoop head. That day, Billy got him back with bat breaker. He set off to make baseball the only sport. Baller Jr found out and followed him. Billy had no idea. Behind Billy's back Baller used his ultimate move, basketball shooter and saved the world...

Rio Rajack (9)
Three Bridges Primary School, Three Bridges

Ticklebottom Has A Friend

There was a monster called Ticklebottom. He was a happy one. He wanted to make a friend but everyone was running away. He tried to blow bubbles from his mouth. It still did not work. Ticklebottom felt sad because he had nobody to play with. He slept overnight, watching the stars. The next day, Ticklebottom went to his house all by himself, wishing he could make a friend. He went to another place. All the children were scared except one. She dragged Ticklebottom into her house. They watched a movie together. They had lots of fun. Ticklebottom was happy.

Delroy Tewe (7)
Three Bridges Primary School, Three Bridges

Zombie

Once upon a time, there lived a strange monster named Velloit. No one liked him because he couldn't fly. That night, he wished to be human. When he woke up, he was human! He was on Earth. But he was a monster again! He went underground with a...

"What's that?" said Velloit. Velloit got closer but it was a zombie! It snatched his tail. He chased it, flying. The zombie was really fast. It took hours to get him. Velloit finally caught him. The zombie ran into a volcano. He released with a *whoosh!* He got his tail back.

Ashley Retter (8)

Three Bridges Primary School, Three Bridges

The Monster From The Underworld

One sunny day, a monster named *Moles* found out that a new villain had travelled down the city of the underworld to destroy it. In his raging madness, Moles turned into a giant and marched to the lair which he crunched with his fist. The villain ran at him with his giant robot. But the robot was no match for the giant Moles. They got into a big fight after which Moles - the giant from the underworld, punched the villain's giant robot. The villain eventually surrendered because he wanted his life spared so he could live to fight again.

Daniel Tanimowo (7)

Three Bridges Primary School, Three Bridges

Cookie And Her Friends

Once upon a time, there was a monster called Cookie. Cookie somehow got sent to this big place with lots of rides. The monster got confused. It said, "Where am I? I hope I'm not lost." So it went off to look around.

"Wow!" It said. "This place is amazing!" So it kind of subtly bumped into this big thing. "Don't hurt me."

"Don't worry. I'm a human. I won't hurt you. Would you like to live with me?"

"I would love to." And they lived happily ever after.

Krupa

Three Bridges Primary School, Three Bridges

Angeliv And Parahell

A long time ago in Parahell, there was a baby named Angeliv. The baby was half demon and half angel and for twenty years they liked each other but one day everything changed. The Demon accidentally opened a portal to the normal world and Angeliv found a kid named Harmony. Harmony didn't like Angeliv hating each other so Harmony said to go back to Parahell. Harmony said that Angeliv had to be nicer and kinder. After a couple of days, they liked each other. After Harmony knew that, they would be friends and help each other when they need it.

Aminata Ndiaye (8)
Three Bridges Primary School, Three Bridges

The Fight Of The Night

Lanster made a friend called Ice Slise. The next day, they got into a fight. At the last moment, someone stopped the fight. To prevent the fight, they moved to a new world. Ice Slise went on Vokason and Lanster was on the planet. Then they found each other and got into another fight. Lanster grabbed a chair and threw it at Ice Slise and he died. Ten years later, Lanster died from old age. Then a fight happened in heaven but they remembered that you can't touch stuff. So they stopped. Then they became friends and played together forever.

Nathan H (8)

Three Bridges Primary School, Three Bridges

Slimey The Hero

One day in Bonkers Land, there were loads of monsters! The main monster is called Slimey. He gets all of the food for the monsters. He's also got a cool trick. When he sticks his tongue out, fire comes off it! There was only one thing they were scared of and it was the monster on the other side of the planet. You would think they would be very nice but they're evil. One day, the bad monster came. Slimey stopped them. He told them, "We should be friends, not enemies." So they now live together happily, never fighting again.

Lily Grimley (8)

Three Bridges Primary School, Three Bridges

The Funny Family

Once upon a time, there was a monster called Alex. He was very cheeky. When he ate he made a mess. The next day he was excited because he was going to a new school. Alex ran down the path. Alex had PE, they did basketball.

Alex came home and went bonkers. He played hide-and-seek. His brother looked everywhere and couldn't find him. Alex said, "Boo!" His brother jumped. It was dinner, they were having beans on toast. He fell asleep for a long time.

On Thursday he broke a plant. He did not tell his mum for a month.

Amirah Shah (8)

Three Bridges Primary School, Three Bridges

Mr Smiggly

Mr Smuggly is a crazy monster. He has red hair and huge horns. He loves to play football with his friends at night-time. One evening, they got spotted by monster hunters. They ran away but forgot their football. The hunters took the football as evidence and to try to trap the monsters. Later, the monsters went back to look for their football. They were sad and scared because the hunters might have seen them. They did! The hunters caught the monsters in a trap, in a big cage and they locked it. The monsters never found their football.

Abhijeet Dale (9)
Three Bridges Primary School, Three Bridges

The King Steals A Missing Child

One day, there was a Bonkers Monster called Bobby, he lived in New Jersey and he shoots out rotten teeth. Bobby had an enemy called Monster Rookey. Bobby met lots of other Bonkers Monsters and they were sent on a mission! Bobby and his monster friends were in a castle to start the mission. Their mission was to find where the king stole a missing child. The Bonkers Monsters went on their mission. Bobby saw the king running in the forest and the king tripped in the forest and Bobby saved the child and they saved her forever and ever!

Emma Devoil (8)

Three Bridges Primary School, Three Bridges

Doctor Evil

Once, a doctor's office had opened. Someone went in there and was never be seen again. One day, Cloudy got suspicious about it and looked through the window. He saw Mr Doctor putting poison in someone's mouth and throwing them into a cell. Then a UFO crashed into the doctor's office and Cloudy asked if he was okay. He said yes and helped Cloudy capture Dr Evil. They threw him off a skyscraper and he died. Then they ate lots food like pizza, hot dogs and cake. They went into a cosy bed, talked and went to bed quietly.

Leela Withers (8)
Three Bridges Primary School, Three Bridges

Fluffy And The Fire Jewel

Once upon a time, Fluffy's fire jewel went missing. The demons took it. She was losing her powers. She went to find the demons. Then she met Oogabo. Oogabo told Fluffy where to go. Fluffy found her fire jewel but then the demons saw her. But she got away, restored her powers and her family's powers. Then aliens took Oogabo. Fluffy called her bird friends to get Oogabo then they got married and had a daughter called Nora. She started to go to school and made a friend called Milly. They were best friends forever and ever.

Lainey Browne (7)

Three Bridges Primary School, Three Bridges

The Quest To Stop Zach

One time there lived Steve. He had a friend called Zach. One day they went into the forest. Then they found some wolves but Steve could not save them. And Zach was still alive. He named himself the Killer and he wanted revenge. Steve found some new friends and then Zach came and said he had three days until he was going to pour water everywhere because they were paper monsters. Three days later, Zach came back with a glass of water. Steve tried to stop him and caused a fight. Steve kicked him into the water. He dissolved!

Harley Redwood (7)

Three Bridges Primary School, Three Bridges

The Monster Who Paints

Julian is a monster who looks like a famous painter because he holds big paintbrushes in his four hands. The people were scared of him but he was just trying to make people laugh. He wanted to open a shop where people could paint faces but nobody liked him. He made a big sign saying: '*I promise I will be kind and not scare you or send you to outer space*'. The people decided to trust the monster and go to his painting shop. The people liked painting in his shop and eventually they all lived happily ever after.

Jayden Hanna (9)

Three Bridges Primary School, Three Bridges

The Story Of Tragaa

There was a monster called Tragaa. Tragaa lived on Mars and loved it there. Then wonderful Tragaa was playing outside and heard a noise. It was a volcano that splashed lava on him. It made him able to shoot fire out of his mouth. Tragaa then got older and had a son called Zackoo. Zackoo was playing outside and got taken.

Tragaa saw who took him and knew it was Zamoo. Zamoo was very weak. Brave Tragaa remembered where Zamoo lived and found Zackoo.

Tragaa killed Zamoo and got his son out of the cage. He was so happy.

Ayaan Farooque (8)
Three Bridges Primary School, Three Bridges

John And His Magic Monster

Once there was a boy called John and he brought his toy to school. Then a kid said his toy was ugly. John said, "No. It's not."
Then the kid said, "Run!"
After, John got really sad because everyone avoided him. When he got home, he tried to make it look better. Suddenly, it spoke to him. John was so confused. When John went to school, so many people were terrified. Then John made a name for it. Dragon Breath. He saw something on its back and said defeat it. So he went there and defeated it.

Leo Trinidad (8)
Three Bridges Primary School, Three Bridges

Chocolate Vs Evil Chocolate

Once upon a time, there was a monster, me, called Chocolate. My evil twin is called Evil Chocolate and he planned to destroy the world. Then I set off on a mission to stop my evil twin from destroying the world. He's black, red, purple and dark blue.

We meet in the middle of the city. It's a big city and we fight. If he wins he destroys the world. If I win he can't destroy the world. "But I won so you can't destroy the world," I said as I won. "You get kicked out the world. Get out!"

Kenzie Oliver (8)

Three Bridges Primary School, Three Bridges

MooMoo Goes To The Beach

One day MooMoo went on a trip to the beach. Lots of hours passed and the beach was closed. People didn't see him. MooMoo swam to the other island he could see. After a while, MooMoo found a cave and decided to stay there and fell asleep. It was eventually midnight.

The next day, he was starving and desperately wanted to eat. It was morning and it was Sunday and in his monster world, on Sunday the beach closed. He found fish and ate them. He was crying and crying to get out. He heard footsteps and help was there.

Avleen Kaur Wahla (8)
Three Bridges Primary School, Three Bridges

Crazy Mr Crazy

One day, Mr Crazy had a walk in the Amazon. Then, Mr Zorg came, Mr Crazy's enemy. Mr Zorg made fun of him. The next day, Mr Crazy said to himself, "I'll say something rude to him." Mr Zorg came bullying again, then, Mr Crazy said, "You're fat!" It made trees fall. Mr Zorg got very upset and never bullied him again. Whenever he got upset, he got revenge. When he won, he did a crazy dance. He was famous for supporting. He supported Chelsea football club. When they scored, he went very crazy.

Adam Timms (8)

Three Bridges Primary School, Three Bridges

Monster Land And Jellyland

Once upon a time, there was this big monster called Vamber Monster. He's from Monsterland. He came to Jellyland where his enemies were. His enemies are called Vasentome and Desonoma. They stole a crown! Until Vamber found out. He ran to them. He punched them and kicked them and got the crown back. It was broken. Vamber had to go fix it with glue and tape. It was fixed! He ran back and the store was closed. The next morning, he ran back and gave it back. He got a shiny medal. He lived happily and loved it so much.

Yusuf Shah (8)
Three Bridges Primary School, Three Bridges

The Cheeky Monster

Cheeky is very cheeky, he is also not very nice. One day, he was bullying someone, but no one could help him because cheeky was very mean. But one day, he changed. He was nice. Nobody could believe it. Everyone was happy because everyone wanted to play with him, but everyone thought he would bully them. On that day, he was so popular, he couldn't even breathe, but he had an enemy, his name was Shuba. Let me tell you how they used to be friends, Cheeky could read minds so he read Shuba's mind and found out.

Aaminah Akiyas (8)
Three Bridges Primary School, Three Bridges

Amia And Cosmo

One day in the city lived a creature called Cosmo. Cosmo was a kind monster. Then one day she saw a girl. She looked sad. So Cosmo went to go see what was wrong. She said those boys always made fun of her. Cosmo said to stand up for herself and be brave. So she went to the boys and said, "Why do you make fun of me?"

"None of your business," said the boys.

So the next day, Cosmo said to ignore the boys because "You are brave and strong and creative so believe in yourself."

Tanisha Bhimjiani (8)

Three Bridges Primary School, Three Bridges

Mr Creepy

There was a monster called Mr Creepy. Mr Creepy was born in Hell and he wanted to escape Hell. Plus, he was an orphan. He was able to escape by making a portal. He came to a place called Crawley. He went on a colossal rampage and asked, "Why did you lock me up in the fiery Hell?" The Marvel heroes tried to lure it near a volcano that was going to erupt every minute. It was going mad. Mr Creepy was tricked. The heroes said it was hot sauce, but Mr Creepy exploded from the volcano. Everyone celebrated.

Owais Rahman (8)
Three Bridges Primary School, Three Bridges

George The Monster Inventor

In the lands of Cornwall, there was a monster named George. He wanted to be an inventor. One day, he wanted to sign his invention up for the contest. It was in London and since George lived far from it, he had to sign his flying bicycle up to get there. Once he arrived in the room with the judges, he didn't make it just because he was a monster. He found a friend named Cyril, who helped him make an advert for his invention. He then got a letter saying that he was a professional, qualified monster inventor.

Harjit Thiagarajan (9)
Three Bridges Primary School, Three Bridges

The Monster Story

Once upon a time, there lived a monster called Amy. She had a friend called Sophie. Sophie had a boyfriend called Jack. Jack was evil but Sophie didn't know, but Amy knew. One day, Amy had a sleepover at Sophie's house. Jack went to Amy's room and tried to kill Amy, but Sophia came, finding Jack. Sophie asked, "Why are you here? I heard a noise so I came to check." After a few months, in December, Amy and Jack got into a fight, Jack died the day after. Soon after, Amy got married to Sim.

Sothia

Three Bridges Primary School, Three Bridges

Monster Fight

Sam was the supreme monster. Every monster was afraid of him. He was supreme at fighting so he protected the city of Yin. It was a Chinese city. Sam had a hoverboard. He was great at hoverboarding so he also taught monsters how to use a hoverboard. He had an enemy, it was the Dark Lord. He could control Sam's hoverboard. It was so annoying. He once got controlled at hoverboard training, it was so annoying and embarrassing. So he stopped using his hoverboard. His enemy, the Dark Lord, was so annoying.

Alexander Nosenko (8)
Three Bridges Primary School, Three Bridges

The Jelly Gem

The Jelly King sent the Jelly Monster to get the Jelly gem that could save the lives of the Jellies. Jelly Monster set off. He went through rain and sun, desert and forest. After days and nights, he finally did it. He had found the Jelly temple with the Jelly gem inside. He saw it, the Jelly gem but it was guarded. Jelly Monster had a plan. So Jelly Monster stuck to the wall and grabbed the Jelly gem. He saw an opening in the ceiling. He jumped out. He rushed home as fast as he could, pleasing the King.

Finn Rina
Three Bridges Primary School, Three Bridges

Fried Crispy

Today I was playing with my little sister. Next, I went to go and get a glass of water in the house. After that, I rang my parents and they came ASAP. When they got home, they called 999 and told them what happened. Later, my monster heard a helicopter and he saw my sister so he chased it. Next, it took him to an island with hundreds of dinosaurs and caves. Later, my monster snuck up on them and couldn't see her. Next, he saw a huge dinosaur standing by a huge cave. So he scared the dinosaur away.

Jacob Drummond (7)
Three Bridges Primary School, Three Bridges

What Is That Sound?

On Monday, I was playing in the forest with my friends. Then we heard someone's noise and we didn't know who it was. Then we climbed up and it was a monster and we ran as fast as we could. Then we told the people and they didn't care. Then one day, we climbed up, they only found the monster. Then we realised that he was scared of us. Then we found we could be friends and we asked him and he nodded his head and we thought he said yes. "Then every day we will come to see you."

Aizan Ailaz (7)
Three Bridges Primary School, Three Bridges

Queen Of Slime

Once upon a time, there lived a queen called the Queen of Slime and the queen lived in a city called The Slime City. She had powers that makes more slime appear and when she was doing it, she saw a bad guy called The Slime Stealer. The Slime Stealer saw the queen and ran away. The queen saw him and went after him and made more slime appear. After a few hours, she went back home to her slime house and looked out the window and saw him stealing all the slime. She ran outside and made more slime.

Freya Sharman (7)
Three Bridges Primary School, Three Bridges

Fluffy Bear Had So Much Fun

Today my bonkers monster is going to do her favourite things that she can do. Next, she will do eating her favourite food. But on Wednesday, Fluffy Bear will also do her favourite song. On Thursday, she is going to a party. On the last day, she is at the park and on Saturday, she is in the swimming pool. Finally, will do musical instruments. Play your piano, violin and trumpet. She walked to play mini games. Today Fluffy Bear will sit at the window. There are some birds. To football, she went.

Kayla Laignau (7)
Three Bridges Primary School, Three Bridges

The Ice Cream Guy

Once upon a time, there was a monster called Ice Cream Boy who loved ice cream. He lived in Ice Cream World. His head was an ice cream machine of ice cream. People didn't eat ice cream like him. He asked someone if he could let him be the governor or he would kill him. He said everybody had to eat ice cream or die. There was a guy that liked lollies and he wanted to be governor, but the ice cream guy killed him and after ten years, died. There was a new governor who also liked ice cream.

Muhammad Abdullah (9)
Three Bridges Primary School, Three Bridges

Wolf Killer's Family

I'm Wolf Killer. I had a nice family. It was ruined by Oscar. Oscar killed my mum. Dad started to act weird. I was angry and tried to kill Oscar.
The next morning my dad was staring at me, it frightened me. I was angry and told him why. I know how it feels when you lose someone. I said, "You're not scary." Then he showed his sharp claws and I showed mine. He showed his sharp teeth and I showed mine. We became best friends and when he gets hungry I will make him steak.

Amelia Gillam (8)
Three Bridges Primary School, Three Bridges

Monster Saver

Once upon a time, there lived a good monster named Withernether in the Nether. One day, his friend was turned into a bad guy by a guy named Blaze. After several days of searching for his friend, he found his friend was a bad guy who lived in the Nether fortress. He knew Blaze could've only done this. To cure his friend, he needed to kill Blaze. He found Blaze and was scared to see him. He won after a long fight with his lasers. Then his friend was cured, and they lived happily together.

Ritojit Mukhopadhyay (8)

Three Bridges Primary School, Three Bridges

The Missing Friend

One day, there was a monster called Cilo Electric. He and his best friend went hunting for food. But while they were hunting... his friend got taken by a strange, mysterious monster. Cilo Electic needed to follow it so he geared up and he followed it to a mysterious jungle. While he was walking, he got stuck in vines. Lightning came out of his eyes. So he shocked the vines and ran very, very fast. He found a small house and ran inside. When he was in, he saw his friend and saved him safely.

Mika Rifky Mohamed (8)
Three Bridges Primary School, Three Bridges

Holiday

Hi, my name is Frizzy and I'm with my friend Spikes. I'm trying to go on holiday but this girl called Lizzy keeps stopping me because her family likes me.

I've just been kicked off an aeroplane and now me and Spikes are trapped on an island. The upside of being on an island is that I can bounce. The bad side is Spikes is going crazy.

It has now been one month. We haven't been saved.

Two months have passed.

Three months have passed. We have finally been saved!

Ashley Ditzel (8)
Three Bridges Primary School, Three Bridges

There Was A Monster Called Destroyer

In a land called Kobis Land, there was a monster called Destroyer. The monster had abilities, when he coughs he turns invisible. For some reason, a city that had King Kong was the monster's enemy. Even though he was helping them. The city got ready to kill the monster. But it was the opposite. They all died, but they were reborn. They got all their stuff and ran! They kept running. Then they geared up better. Then they chopped off the monster's legs. Then they chopped the heart...

Nathan Bottazzini
Three Bridges Primary School, Three Bridges

Sacku And The Monkey King

There was a monster called Sacku. He lived in a forest with his family. Every night, they would sleep in a small cave. One day, Sacku came home with a chest he had found. A few days later, he started to fly and shoot lasers. That night, his mum and dad were injured and the treasure was taken. His parents pointed Sacku towards where the thief went. With the wings Sacku had grown, he flew to the thief. Easy, it was a king. But Sacku aimed perfectly and shot it in the eye. Then he went home.

Sam Patel (7)

Three Bridges Primary School, Three Bridges

Mr Confused

Mr Confused was walking in the jungle. In a small swamp was a small hut. A witch came out and splashed a potion. Mr Confused lost all his memory. He woke up in a tree and saw a book. He aimed up and got it. He read it, then came a monster called Mr Beast. Mr Confused ran and read the book in a cave. He did all the stuff and became a full god. He found Mr Beast and slaughtered him, everyone cheered. Mr Confused opened a portal and entered it. Everyone wanted to go to the portal peacefully.

Sarunya Thamilmaran (8)
Three Bridges Primary School, Three Bridges

Manter

Once upon a time, there was a monster named Manter, and Manter's dream was to be a footballer. When he grew up, that was what he did and he signed up for a tournament. He trained for a long time and it was time for the tournament. He and his team met their arch-enemy, Raknor. He was good at football. The match had started, both teams were good, but Manter scored and scored again until his team had five goals. They won! As Manter went to claim his reward, he was so happy and joyful.

Morgan Myburgh (8)
Three Bridges Primary School, Three Bridges

Mr Masty

Once upon a time, there was a monster called Mr Masty. He stayed at Dragonworld and he could breathe fire and turn stones into toys, they were his skills and tricks. His enemy was the fire dragon. Mr Masty wished he could fly, but needed to do training, so he kept doing it. He could fly a little bit. When he grew up, he had to fight the fire dragon. Mr Masty defeated the fire dragon by putting ice on his body. After, when Mr Masty grew, he said, "My dream has come true, yay!"

Yavan Murugaraj (9)
Three Bridges Primary School, Three Bridges

Ronk's Mission To Space

Once upon a time, there was a monster called Ronk. Ronk liked to travel to space. He really liked to play rounders outside. One day, he walked so far that he found a rocket. This was his chance to enter space. He snuck to the rocket launcher. The rocket opened its door and he entered the rocket. As soon as he noticed that he was floating in the air, he reached the moon. The world was a sight. Then, it was time for Ronk to return to Earth with a smile. After, he was very, very happy.

Nithin Nadane (8)

Three Bridges Primary School, Three Bridges

Scary Robot Monster

This monster came alive from a robot toy. He was scary but very friendly and a bit sad because whenever he tried making some friends they all went away. His wish was to have a friend. Someone came down from the sky. They saw him and they became friends and everyone started to like him. He became a nice monster and helpful. That day he helped all the people. From that day I was happy. From that day on everyone thought he was the happiest and the best. From that day on he was happy.

Eman Aijaz (7)
Three Bridges Primary School, Three Bridges

The Plabob Island!

Once upon a time, there was a boy named Bloblob. He lived on an island called Plabob Land. He had amazing people on the island and his enemies were people that do not live on his island. It was the next day and he went on his balcony and Bloblob saw so many planes. He saw people that do not look like him and he noticed they do not belong on the island. He was freaking out. He thought he could put a big shield around the castle and it worked. Now he was the only one on the island.

Kaidee Hanna
Three Bridges Primary School, Three Bridges

Meanie

Once upon a time, there was a monster called Meanie. She was a nice girl but she had evil powers. She was planning to take over the world. But the superheroes came. Then they helped save the world. They were defeating the monster. The little monster didn't give up, and with her icy powers, she got back up and started defeating people again. The superheroes didn't give up and the little monster dropped and cried. The superheroes cuddled her and lived happily ever after.

Surriyah-Rose Jock Miller (8)
Three Bridges Primary School, Three Bridges

Bonky On Earth

On a dark day in outer space, lived an alien called Bonky. He lived with his mum and dad. Everyone was asleep except Bonky. He saw his dad's ship. He went in and looked. Bonky turned it on. It went to Earth. The ship crashed on a field. Bonky walked out of the ship and saw the Earth. Bonky walked and walked and then he saw a group of children talking. He went to them but they ran away. A few hours later, they said sorry to Bonky. They made a ship and he went back home.

Maayah Jameela Khan (8)
Three Bridges Primary School, Three Bridges

Dobby And Cosemo

One sunny day, a monster called Dobby went to the city and he made everyone laugh except one monster Cosemo. When he saw me, he put me in jail. I thought of plans for days but none worked. So I decided to think up the best plan I had. When I got the plan, I wanted to put it into action. Suddenly, the monster came to check on me. He stepped on the drain that I covered in mud and he fell down the drain! The keys fell right to my feet so I unlocked the gate and went home.

Milan Kadar (8)

Three Bridges Primary School, Three Bridges

Dunkdevil And The Boy

There once was a creature that no one had seen before. He was called Dunkdevil. He was evil. He made it to the mainland and scared everyone. He then destroyed everything on Earth. Then the monster saw that it was bad and he stopped being bad and became good. But in the last second, he fell off a cliff and nearly died. No one heard from him again until one day a boy found him at the bottom of a cliff and helped him to get better. They became best friends forever.

Harry Makepeace (8)

Three Bridges Primary School, Three Bridges

Cotton Candy

Once upon a time, there was a monster called Cotton Candy. He lived in Monsterland. He loved playing with his friends and his friends called him a crybaby. He hated it so he said, "I am not your friend anymore," but he had no friends anymore. He was sad, so sad that he said, "I want friends again."

His friends said, "Sorry, we won't say you're a crybaby anymore."

Now they are happy and live happily together.

Anastasia Eleonore (9)
Three Bridges Primary School, Three Bridges

Bonny Goes Back To Space

There was a monster named Bonny. He was very kind but somehow no one wanted to be his friend. He lived in space with other monsters. Abruptly, he landed in the city where people live! People saw him and ran away straight away. His skill was going fast so he wins any race and he ran after them, far away from space, nowhere back! He wandered in the woods when Bonny heard a howl! A wolf walked up behind him and began a fight. Bonny saw a ship and flew off.

Aimee Murray (7)
Three Bridges Primary School, Three Bridges

Star Light

Once upon a time, a monster called Star Light left her world and she grew. She decided to find a kind queen. She came down to Earth. She saw a giant castle. She went inside and saw something above her. It was a trap! She went over to it and saw a big gold door and tried to open it but it was locked. She went outside the castle and saw the queen with keys. Oh no, this queen was bad! So Star Light hid behind her and killed her at once! Defeated!

Zainab Farooq (7)
Three Bridges Primary School, Three Bridges

Sweet Tooth Panther

One day, there was a monster called Panther. He lived in Candy Land. Later that day, Panther went to the dentist that said he needed to eat fewer sweets and brush his teeth. Later, Panther said he was going to brush his teeth for ten minutes. He did, but it wasn't enough. Then he went too far, he brushed his teeth for one hour. The next day, Panther went to the dentist and told them to remove his teeth. They did and they grew back better.

Galiene Natalie Sebide (8)
Three Bridges Primary School, Three Bridges

Saving My Dad

Once upon a time, Sparkle Bomb lived in a little candy land. She loves karate and swimming. The king was her enemy. He killed her mum and sister. They lived just two of them. One day, she went for a walk. She saw the king putting her dad in jail. She didn't know why. She overheard the king saying, "I will break your mint house down." She used a bat and killed the king. They found her mum and sister and lived happily ever after.

Lamya Razi Mohamed (7)
Three Bridges Primary School, Three Bridges

The Wolf That Got Famous

There was a wolf called Scar. He was mostly bullied so he wasn't popular... His bullies pulled his tail! Scar wasn't happy... One day Scar wasn't himself. He failed his training. He loved training! The bullies worried so they went and asked if he was okay. Eventually, they became friends and was a secret for a bit. Later he became famous without even knowing that his old bullies were famous! So they lived happily ever after.

Eliza Iotu (8)

Three Bridges Primary School, Three Bridges

Evil Derilyi

A long time ago in an egg there lived a creature named Evil Derilyi. He did not have any skills or tricks and its enemy was a strong horse. It was so big. It tried to kill him. Evil Derilyi ran into a deep, dark, gloomy forest. He stayed there for many months.

Twelve months had gone by. "I do not have a friend." He got out. He saw lots of little creatures. A girl monster was named Evil Sweet. And they became friends.

Timea Kery-Toth (8)
Three Bridges Primary School, Three Bridges

Body Hunter

The monster says, "Where?" People don't know where it is and are looking. Caleb finds out it is looking for something but doesn't know what. He finds a legend of its life. He finds out it's looking for its body. He locates a temple but there are guards so he fights like his hands are blades and wins a kill. He sees a statue of a body so he brings it back to the monster. It puts it on and leaves in peace.

Caleb Thorn (8)

Three Bridges Primary School, Three Bridges

Grob And The Balloon

Once upon a time, there was a monster called Grob. He really wanted to learn to fly. He had this one red balloon which he thought he would fly. One day, he woke up and thought this was the day to fly. He took his red balloon and climbed to the top of the tree. Hoping the red balloon would make him fly and holding tight to the red balloon, he jumped.
It did not work! "Ouch!" he shouted.

Zayn Amin (8)
Three Bridges Primary School, Three Bridges

Tear Hair

One gloomy night, when a neighbourhood was asleep, Tear Hair broke into people's houses. He tore their hair out. One day, he spotted his enemy, Shazaz. She was the opposite of Tear Hair. She went around making people pretty. Tear Hair wanted to team up with her. "I don't want to be a part of your team," shouted Shazaz. From that day, they were grateful friends and helpful people.

Mia Roper (9)
Three Bridges Primary School, Three Bridges

My Friend Was Gone!

Once upon a time, I had my best friend called Finn. I was from Athens, he was from Jelly Land. One day, my best friend Finn was gone. I saw him, he is with my enemies. I used my power of invisibility to help to save him. I got my army to help him as well. My army got him without my enemies looking. I played with my friend Finn forever. He came to my house for a sleepover with me.

Mahi
Three Bridges Primary School, Three Bridges

The Big Monster

In a land far away a huge dragon came out behind the trees. The monster had six eyes and it was so big. Then it destroyed the town with fireballs but it saw me. It came down and I had my sword with my bow. But it didn't kill me, so I put my bow down. Then it lay down. Then I got on it and we flew away and we were friends.

Lacey (8)
Three Bridges Primary School, Three Bridges

Jude

In a creek, there lived a monster called Jude. He was a friendly monster but one day, a herd of villagers came. Jude's mum took him away but Jude's dad stayed behind. Jude and his mum tried to find safety.

Two years passed. Jude got older. Jude started to regret the incident.

Max Roper (8)
Three Bridges Primary School, Three Bridges

Hulk And The Destroying Of London

A monster called Hulk has a whole city to destroy but he can't do it alone. Hulk gets some of his friends to help. Hulk and his friends get to London and start setting everything on fire.

Twelve hours later, the city is theirs. Hulk builds it up again and then Hulk rules England.

Robbie Irving (8)

Three Bridges Primary School, Three Bridges

Gloomy Monster

It all started with a monster who was gloomy. He could not find a friend to play with. He was sad and bumped into another monster. He was sad and clumsy. They chatted about how they felt. They became friends and were playing tag. Then they finished playing and wanted to play tomorrow.

Zaine-King Burrows (7)

Three Bridges Primary School, Three Bridges

Phantom

Once upon a time, there was a boy called Jeff who was friends with a monster called Bob. But once, they got into a fight and Bob chopped off Jeff's head.

Lenny Kemsley (7)
Three Bridges Primary School, Three Bridges

Maximus Glutimus And The Plot To Defeat Professor Gloop

Max jumped on the skateboard. He knew his mission, to stop the mischievous Professor Gloop. "Take me to Professor Gloop's base," said Max. "Navigating route," the computer beeped. Within seconds, his flying skateboard shot off into the galaxy.

Meanwhile, Professor Gloop was getting ready for Max to burst in out of nowhere. "3, 2, 1..." Professor Gloop told himself. Max burst in right on time. "Ah, there you are. I thought I was going to count to three a few more times," Professor Gloop said.

"Hi, nice machine you got here!" Max exclaimed. Max had already saved the day. "Sword time!"

Harley Bladen-Hayes (10)
Uplands Junior School, Wolverhampton

Kidnapped

Dear Diary,

Pupple here! Today, I left Starford House and headed for Kelpie Forest. Abruptly, a mysterious scent bewildered my three noses... Seahorses! From behind me, a hooded creature clasped me. Black... Darkness...

When I awoke I was in a dark, enclosed cell. Panic-stricken, I desperately searched for an exit. None... I instantly knew what was happening; the seahorses had captured me in an endeavour to force me to work forever.

From out of nowhere, a young, friendly-looking seahorse approached, mumbling, "Sorry," like a mouse. The barred door opened and I rapidly thanked her before whirling into the distance. Freedom.

Elsa McMurtrie (11)

Uplands Junior School, Wolverhampton

Lost In LA

Addie was a normal monster, roaming the streets of LA. When she was on 'Street Mavis' a smaller monster popped out of nowhere, Maya. Maya distracted Addie, turning down tiny streets and through mini cracks.

At last, they stopped. "Where are we?" questioned Addie multiple times.

"I don't know!" replied Maya, a bit too protectively. Addie started searching around, looking for any sign of what road they were on. Slipping through the cracks was easy but getting out that was a challenge! Squeezing her way through, Addie found herself in what was called 'Southward Street'. Home? Was it or not?

Martha Taylor-Ashcroft (10)
Uplands Junior School, Wolverhampton

From The Box Under My Bed

"Roar!"

What shall I do? I thought. A large noise was coming from the box under my bed. *Should I open it?* I thought. Just then, I decided to lift up the box. "Roar!" it went.

"Aargh!"

It was a large monster with three eyes and four heads! I ran downstairs and told my mum, brother and sister. My dad heard us and came racing up but then the monster said, "Can you be my friend?"

"What shall I say?" I asked Dad.

"Say yes," said Dad.

I said yes and then we all lived together forever and we're happy.

Charlie Moulsdale (10)
Uplands Junior School, Wolverhampton

Pinkachoo And Me

Suddenly, a weird-looking creature appeared in my room. I said, "Hello?"

She said, "Hello, I'm Pinkachoo! I'm from Pink Planet in a different universe. I've got teleportation powers but they're new to me and I need to get home."

In a flash we teleported to Italy! She said, "Sorry" but I didn't care, I loved it! She said we needed to get home so we went on a mission to find a key that led to a door.

We finally found it after days. She waved goodbye and went home. I felt sad. Unusually, it was just a dream.

Ava Rutter (10)

Uplands Junior School, Wolverhampton

The Adventures Of Bonkerina

One gloomy morning, Bonkerina woke up to go to school. It was very rainy but she was a very cheerful monster. She walked every miserable morning to Uplands Monster School. "Oh, I wish monsters understood me like they do here." She walked through the gates and went to class. Her first lesson was English but it was science week so the work was in science books. After maths, playtime began so she went outside. She loved break until St Bonkerus appeared and after many hours of getting him to leave, Bonkerina did it. The school blessed her with rainbow powers.

Laila Montague (8)
Uplands Junior School, Wolverhampton

My Mysterious Bedroom Monster

It's 8pm, Jake's bedtime. Jake walks up the stairs, then snuggles into his bed. It is now 1am, Jake wakes up because he can hear mysterious noises coming from underneath his bed. Jake gets worried so he turns the light on but there isn't anything there, so Jake turns the light off and falls back to sleep.

Under the bed, Blake is trying to sleep but someone just turned the light on. Blake is scared that there is a monster in his room.

Jake does not know about Blake. Blake doesn't know about Jake. Which one is the bedroom monster?

Mason Russello-Nar (9)
Uplands Junior School, Wolverhampton

Peace Or War?

There once was a monster named Belchy Fuz who lived happily on his planet named Scaely Bogey Planet. Sadly, this so-called happiness would not last for long. When he was only three monster years (also known as six human years) another planet named Fiery Flame attacked. They had weapons unimaginable and most of them were... fire-themed.

Sent to Earth, which was on the other side of the galaxy, in a pod, Fuz spent ten monster years in space until he unexpectedly landed with a bump. As you would, he opened the door in wonder as a human appeared!

Sienna Kumari (10)
Uplands Junior School, Wolverhampton

It's Not Me, It's My Basement

Bang! I had only heard this once. *Bang! Bang! Bang!* Five years ago. At this point, I had lost all my sanity so I got out of bed, went downstairs and opened the basement door. To my horror, there was blood everywhere, the sandwiches I'd been feeding it and bones. I walked down a long, winding corridor that twisted and turned until I got to a dead end. There it was, the monster, only it looked like me! It had my pyjamas, my hair, except its face had hollow eyes and a split mouth that said, "You're next, Kelly."

Lucy Amelia Brown (10)
Uplands Junior School, Wolverhampton

The Legendary Discovery

One awful night, Tom woke up at 3am to find a banging noise under his bed. At first, he thought it was a dream so he pinched himself but it wasn't a dream... Tom, slowly and cautiously, crept off his bed to find an ugly, snot-green monster with fangs like kitchen knives quickly drooling.

Suddenly, Tom got a sturdy baseball bat and with all his strength, whacked the ugly thing. For a moment, he thought it was dead but it was merely just wounded. So, with all the knowledge he got from magic books, he created a vortex...

Carrum Sekhon (9)

Uplands Junior School, Wolverhampton

My New Pet

I got home and went to Osnay's house. She had rules. One, don't wear shoes in the house. Two, don't open the wooden cupboard behind the front door. I said okay and she left to get some popcorn. I, however, didn't, and opened the wooden cupboard and flipped the light switch on and walked down the cold, stone stairs. At the bottom, there was a box. I opened it and found a monster with the name Beeny the Buttercup. I took it home and kept it safe. It is pink and rainbow and it lives under my comfy, big bed.

Jasmin Sandhu (9)
Uplands Junior School, Wolverhampton

The Lost Monster

Under my bed, while I was tidying up, I found a little monster with wide eyes. He came out and I saw he was pink and spotty with a short, stripy tail. I could tell he was from a different planet from his appearance. "I'm lost," he whispered.

So I started searching around my room, looking for old things. Then I started building; I glued bits together. It was a rocket and I took it outside. The cold air blew my hair. Carefully, I placed him on top slowly. I said goodbye and waved to him as he flew away.

Beatrice Machin (9)

Uplands Junior School, Wolverhampton

Lulu's Competition

All of a sudden, a bright pink monster with a light pink tongue popped out of an enormous teacup just like popcorn. Lulu was not a scary monster but a nice and friendly one. She had been endeavouring to get a golden trophy for skipping. Two months later, it was the day! Lulu's heart was beating as fast as a bass drum. She wanted to get this over with because she did not enjoy this intense feeling. In the end, she won! When she got back home she put it on her dusty, old shelf. Lulu admired it.

Acira Kumar (9)
Uplands Junior School, Wolverhampton

Teddy In The Basement

One day there was a little girl called Lily and a little boy called Max and they were playing with a bouncy ball. Then it went into the basement and nobody likes the basement. They went down the stairs and they heard a very strange noise. It sounded like a cat mixed with a dog. They looked at each other in confusion, they thought it was an old teddy that had been chucked down there. They walked down the stairs, slowly turned on the light and they saw a ball of fluff, no, a monster!

Jessica Morgan
Uplands Junior School, Wolverhampton

The Monster Under My Bed

Under my bed, I found a minuscule rainbow monster with three rainbow eyes. On its back were wings and a pearly white unicorn horn! It was a pegasus monster! I slowly opened my hand for it to crawl onto. It was so fluffy when I stroked it! I thought about it for a while. It was not mine to keep though, was it? I thought that I would keep it for just one night and I would let it in the wild tomorrow morning. It was not a pain at all! I fed it bread quickly and let it go.

Aadreyi Chattopadhyay (9)
Uplands Junior School, Wolverhampton

Stuck On Earth

One night when I got in bed my pillow was m-m-moving! I threw the pillow at the wall and there was a ball of fluff? And it talked! It said, "Help me!" It was asking for help so I asked what help it needed. It said, "Stuck on Earth."

"I can help," I said, comforting it.

So two days later, I built a big slingshot and said goodbye and the alien was saved.

Lewis Hitch (10)

Uplands Junior School, Wolverhampton

Fluffball And The Goblin

Fluffball was a kind monster who lived in Sprinkle City. One sunny day, she saw an old Goblinysplob and said, "I will help you!"

"Thank you," replied the Goblinysplob.

Fluffball knew she had done the right thing. She knew you had to be kind to be a better person. Everybody should be kind, respectful and happy. Even monsters can be kind so if they can, you can!

Georgia Winwood (8)

Uplands Junior School, Wolverhampton

Wiggly Wings

One day there was a little monster called Wiggly Wings. Another monster was jealous of his wings so when he was asleep he took Wiggly Wings' wings and put them on himself.
But the next day they were gone and he was told to leave. Moral: Don't take what is not yours.

Abigail Shepherd (8)
Uplands Junior School, Wolverhampton

Young Writers Information

We hope you have enjoyed reading this book – and that you will continue to in the coming years.

If you're a young writer who enjoys reading and creative writing, or the parent of an enthusiastic poet or story writer, do visit our website **www.youngwriters.co.uk**. Here you will find free competitions, workshops and games, as well as recommended reads, a poetry glossary and our blog. There's lots to keep budding writers motivated to write!

If you would like to order further copies of this book, or any of our other titles, then please give us a call or order via your online account.

Young Writers
Remus House
Coltsfoot Drive
Peterborough
PE2 9BF
(01733) 890066
info@youngwriters.co.uk

Join in the conversation!
Tips, news, giveaways and much more!

 **YoungWritersUK**    **YoungWritersCW**   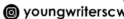 **youngwriterscw**